THEY CALLED HIM THE POISONED FROG

He was the worst, the most brutal of all the Korean guard commanders. They called him the Poisoned Frog.

He looked up into Van Reebek's face with contemptuous amusement. Van Reebek had dared to challenge him—now he was going to pay for it.

The Poisoned Frog took his bayonet out of its scabbard and stuck it in the ground. Then he took the scabbard out of its frog. It was solid leather tipped with metal, but flexible.

Van Reebek took a deep breath and thanked God that there was a limit to the amount of pain that can be borne and prayed that he would reach that limit quickly.

JOHN WYLLIE

SURVIVAL

CORGI BOOKS
A DIVISION OF TRANSWORLD PUBLISHERS

SURVIVAL

A CORGI BOOK

Originally published in Great Britain
by Martin Secker & Warburg Ltd.
under the title *The Goodly Seed*

PRINTING HISTORY
Secker & Warburg Edition published 1953
Secker & Warburg Third Impression 1954
Corgi Edition published 1957
Corgi Edition reprinted 1959
Corgi Edition reissued 1966

This book is set in
10 pt. Garamond

Corgi Books are published by Transworld Publishers Ltd.,
Bashley Road, London, N.W.10.
Made and printed in Great Britain by
Hunt Barnard & Co. Ltd., Aylesbury, Bucks.

FOR
SONJA

PART ONE

—

December 23rd, 1944

CHAPTER I

THE landing barge moved quickly across the half-mile of water that separated the small island from the mainland. Although it was only eight o'clock, the morning air was saturated with a heat that constrained breathing and slowed movement to the pace of a man walking in deep water.

Lieutenant Van Reebek, in charge of the boat's cargo of prisoners of war, felt suffocated by the warmth and smell that rose from the densely packed, half-naked men around him. The foetid air that travelled in a block with the boat left a sour taste across his palate. The touch of his neighbour's moist bare arm against his own made him recoil and shudder as if from contact with something loathsome. Half-heartedly he tried to argue himself into the belief that because the skin of the man next to him was white he should have no cause to feel repelled when it met his. Unhappily, the thought led him up a false trail to the memory of a remark he had heard the British Camp Commandant make one day. The old man had said, roundly and damningly:

"If a man has native blood in him, I can tell it the moment he starts to sweat."

Van Reebek had never been able to make up his mind whether the Commandant had known he was within earshot when he spoke.

Van Reebek's great-grandfather had married a Javanese woman. Van Reebek knew that the slight duskiness of his complexion and the black hair which he had inherited from his mother, in conjunction with his Dutch blue eyes, were not sufficient to identify him as a half-caste. But perhaps the smell of his skin . . .

Van Reebek shrugged; and dismissing this anxiety from his mind, he allowed another and much greater one to take its place.

As the boat drew nearer to the island shore, he looked over

the heads of the men crowded in front of him and fixed his eyes on the hut which served the Japanese Command as a guard-house. Stretching towards him, the reflection of some tall coco-nut palms that stood round the hut moved blackly on the still water, like the weaving legs of a spider.

Clearing his working-party past the camp guard was always the final test for which, after each night's work on the airfield, he had to hold back some special reserve of nervous strength. Each night he set out with his men like a man running a mile race, knowing that his success or failure would depend entirely on the amount of drive he had been able to hold back for the last burst that would bring him to the finishing line.

It was a race in which the handicapping had been unfairly imposed and was against him from the start. Ever since the first day of his captivity his height and size had made him conspicuous. They offered a challenge to the camp guards, none of whom ever stood more than head high to his armpit.

"They love taking the mike out of you, Van Reebek," the Commandant had explained one day, "because they can give expression to their hatred for you as a member of a race which is their declared enemy. As common soldiers, it gives them great pleasure to be able to insult and beat a representative of a class that is their instinctive enemy. Finally, they can humble one, a giant by their standards, comparable to their own tribe of giant wrestlers, who is unarmed and forbidden to strike back."

Van Reebek had overcome his fear of their ordinary sport —of being made to kneel so that his face was brought below the level of his tormentor's and thus within comfortable reach for the face-slapping that would ensue. In these circumstances he had learned to shut himself away, to feel contempt for the man who struck him, to ignore the pain and the humiliation. But . . . if he showed any sign of weakening, of fear, if he said a wrong word, or the interpreter made a faulty translation, then the sport turned to a violence that grew in proportion to the amount of blood drawn by the blows that were aimed at his head and shoulders.

The boat ran softly up on to the sand and the brow was lowered to allow the men ashore.

Most of those who straggled up the sandy apron towards the thickly wooded crown of the island wore only a strip of cloth that covered their genitals and was fastened round their waists

8

with string, a pair of dilapidated boots and a rattan, coolie hat. They were of mixed nationalities, with the Dutch predominating: white Dutch, half-caste Dutch; coloured men from the Dutch East Indies. There were a few British, one or two Chinese, a Turk, an Armenian and an American negro.

The coloured men and the half-castes had stood the degradation of being Japanese prisoners better than the whites. Most of the latter were emaciated, furtive and spiritless, while many of those with darker skins were still well covered, with their natural gaiety and vitality almost undimmed.

Unaccustomed food, surroundings, climate, manual work and subservience to those whom they had traditionally looked upon as a coolie race had taken the sap out of the stringy Europeans who staggered exhaustedly up the beach to fall in, for counting and a search, in front of the guard-house.

Van Reebek checked the number of men in his party, then stepped in front of them to wait for the guard commander to come out. As he stood there, he closed his eyes, willing down upon himself a power of anaesthesia, a power which would deaden his natural fear of physical and nervous pain.

When he opened his eyes again the little yellow man was standing a few paces off looking at him curiously.

Van Reebek called his party to attention and saluted. His salute was returned smartly. Van Reebek relaxed. The expression on the flat, bony face was amiable.

"Hachi ju ku," Van Reebek reported. The guard commander noted the number on a pad, then counted the party himself. He did not arrive at the same figure, but was loath to count again. Counting was an effort; and he suspected that Van Reebek was right. If he raised an objection and was proved wrong it would mean loss of face. So he accepted the count he had been given and was about to dismiss the party when a movement in the rear rank caught his eye.

He picked out the man who had moved and brought him forward to stand by Van Reebek. It was significant that the men in the front rank were mostly coloured or half-castes and that the whites had fallen in under the lee of any violence from the guard that the darker skinned men appeared to provide.

The man who was now beside Van Reebek was gaunt and big-boned, a framework of ridges and angles draped with skin. The mouth was thin and weak, continual hunger had formed deep hollows under the cheek-bones and the small, deep-sunk, dark eyes were restless and nervous. He was European Dutch; his name, Haverkamp. Before his capture he had been the captain of a Dutch merchant ship. He wore a pair of much patched green shorts. He was hatless and barefooted. Round his waist was a thin leather strap: suspended from it was an aluminium water-bottle.

The guard commander put his finger under the bottom of the bottle and raised it a little, testing its weight.

Van Reebek heard a man who stood in the party behind him catch his breath.

After a few seconds' pause the guard commander told Van Reebek to dismiss the rest of the party. At the same time he indicated that Van Reebek and Haverkamp should stay. Then he sent for the interpreter.

Van Reebek was conscious of being watched by the men in the cookhouse, which stood a hundred yards up the slope towards the centre of the island. They had stopped work and were morbidly interested in the scene that experience told them was likely to take place in front of the guard-house.

Van Reebek felt a dull, futile anger rising within him. He wanted to curse Haverkamp for being such a fool as to think that he could get away with smuggling food into the camp in his water-bottle. Then he remembered that the man had very nearly got away with it, and wanted to curse him for drawing attention to himself by moving. But Van Reebek kept silent, partly because the guard commander still stood waiting patiently in front of him, partly because he knew it would be as pointless to curse Haverkamp as it would be to curse the war for having led him into the doubly ridiculous position into which he found he had been thrust. Doubly ridiculous, because he could not seriously be held responsible when a hungry man took risks to get a little extra food and because, as a junior officer in the Dutch army, he was supposed to answer for the discipline of a man old enough to be his father, a sea captain of long standing and of sufficient seniority, had be been in Van Reebek's own service, to be at least a major or colonel.

DeVissar, the interpreter, arrived and saluted.

The Korean sucked air through his teeth, then spoke in a rapid, smooth-flowing babble of words.

"Daa Veesa. Anoné . . . why should a man who is returning, having been twelve hours out of camp, still have a full water-bottle?"

The question was put guilelessly, the tone of voice one of mild interest.

DeVissar repeated the question in Dutch.

For a long time Haverkamp didn't answer. The guard commander waited patiently, his dark aerofoil eyes resting unblinkingly on his victim's face.

Van Reebek turned his head and looked at his fellow countryman. The prominent adam's apple in Haverkamp's throat was bobbing up and down like an erratic piston in its skinny sheath.

Two or three times Haverkamp tried to find his voice. At last he succeeded, and when it came it was whining and wretched.

"I have hunger," he said. "At the airfield I was able to obtain some uncooked rice. Enough to fill my bottle."

The Korean scuffed the toe of his boot in the sand and watched it thoughtfully. Presently he said:

"To obtain rice, this man must have spoken with a Malay or Chinese coolie. That is forbidden. Also he must have traded something for the rice. Ask him what he traded for it."

Haverkamp looked as if he were going to deny having traded anything for it.

Van Reebek said, "Tell the truth."

Haverkamp shrugged:

"My boots," he said.

The Korean narrowed his eyes and looked at the sky. He spoke as if addressing a judge up there on a cloud.

"Boots which were given by Dai Nippon. That is also forbidden and shows ingratitude. Did he know all these things were forbidden?" And it was the interpreter this time who prompted, adding on his own account, "If I were you I should say 'yes'."

Haverkamp looked from the Korean to the interpreter, then round to Van Reebek. Each of them wore an expression of indifference.

"Yes," he said.

The guard commander measured him from the ground up with his eyes and pursed his lips. Finally he held out his hand.

"I will take the bottle and the rice. When I have emptied the bottle, the interpreter will bring it back to you."

Then, with it in his hands, he turned to Van Reebek and told him, quietly, to dismiss.

11

Salutes were again exchanged and Van Reedek and Haver-kamp marched off. They parted at the top of the path without having spoken a word to each other.

The guard commander later gave the rice to the fat Dutch-man who was in charge of the cookhouse, with instructions to include it in the general rations. He made the donation with the air of one making a fine and generous gesture.

The Dutchman took the rice, and that evening cooked it and ate it himself.

2

The man looked at his watch. He lay on a straw mat in the corner of a long, roughly built, wooden barrack that held over two hundred sick and dying men. His face was puffed and bloated and his eyes were deeply set behind thick, swollen lids that concealed any movement of the eye-balls. Watching his eyes and seeing the irises turn to the left or right was like watching a bubble move in a spirit-level.

He had been awake and waiting for over four hours.

He was not in pain, only uncomfortable from being swathed too deeply in the thick swellings of his own flesh: swellings which, when he lay down, came quickly to his face and neck, and when he sat up, went to his shins, ankles and feet. At all times he found that the act of breathing needed a conscious physical effort.

He was waiting for Van Reebek to come in and report.

He was the Camp Commandant, the Englishman, elderly and grizzled, whom Van Reebek had been thinking about in the landing barge.

As he lay, he watched the three sick-bay orderlies doing the little they could for their patients: issuing the double spoonful of wet rice and mug of sugarless tea that was breakfast: helping dysentery cases to stagger like grimacing dolls made of thin sticks and thongs back and forth to the latrine.

One man had thus to be helped every half-hour all through the day and night, and set up a feeble cry for assistance each time.

The bench was six feet wide and ran the full length of the barrack on each side. Between the two rows was a narrow gangway. All along both benches the sick men lay shoulder to shoulder. Among them there was one that lay covered from head to foot with a blanket, one who had died during the night.

The Commandant saw all this and registered it automatically, as the mind of a factory worker registers the production line while it moves endlessly past him.

Sometimes, when the Commandant watched the scene consciously, he laboured to find a design or a purpose behind its repetitive, almost mathematical function.

His first conclusion had been the not very remarkable one that he was watching nature at work in one of her most careless and haphazard moods. To this he had to add that much of the life and vitality that he saw slipping away unused through lack of nourishment, medical care and proper surroundings was material that had in any case been born to be wasted. The only difference was that now it was being disposed of in a bleak, unfriendly setting, in discomfort on hard boards, instrad of on cheap matresses and steel-sprung beds.

But at this moment, at 8.15 a.m. on the 23rd of December, 1944, the Commandant was not concerned with the philosophical reasons for the death and suffering with which he was surrounded. He was thinking of Van Reebek.

The night shift was the most unpopular assignment in the camp: to be officer in charge of it, the most testing job.

It was a far greater strain on worn nerves to work by night than by day. Fear, pain and despair cast more frightening shadows in the flickering, dramatic light of the petroleum flares.

The only two obvious suicides the Commandant had known in nearly three years of internment had occurred on night shift. Men gave up more easily at night because their weakness and shame were hidden. They could cry unseen. They could curse, and their futile grimacing was lost in the darkness.

Of course, the night shift had its advantages too. The Japanese and Korean guards were sleepy and less watchful. Their pulses, like everyone else's, beat slower in the hours before dawn. For those in whom the sap still ran warm, for those who were still sufficiently alive to see advantages and take them, there were unusual possibilities. Contact could be made with the Malay or Chinese coolie labour. If people had money or articles to trade, they could get a little extra food, and news. Unreliable though most of it was, news had a great value. At this date it was almost always good news, almost always news which seemed to bring the day of release a little nearer.

Van Reebek had a contact out in the dark, on the airstrip, with an educated Chinese, forced to do coolie labour to keep his family in food. His information always, eventually, proved to be correct.

Though he thought he was resigned to the idea that he himself was destined to die before he would be released, the Commandant still hoped on for the victory of his people. He also liked to have some cheerful news to hand on to those who came to visit him. To see the quickening of their hope made his own sinking softer and more acceptable.

This was his second war. As a young man he had survived the Gallipoli landings in 1915 but had been wounded in Mesopotamia soon afterwards. As adjutant to an R.A.F. squadron in 1942 he had been flown out to Java from the Middle East just in time to be caught and put behind barbed wire.

The Commandant saw Van Reebek come through the door at the far end of the hut and pushed himself slowly into a more upright position to receive him.

3

"It was lucky that Tanaka was the guard commander," said the Commandant. "It was also lucky that Haverkamp took DeVissar's advice. That's the worst of a Mission training for an Oriental, they only add to their own morality those bits of ours that they find useful."

Van Reebek didn't understand.

"Tanaka was trained at a Mission. He is a Christian. It was probably the same Mission we used to support with our pennies when I was a schoolboy. There was a collection for it every Sunday. The missionaries teach their converts the importance of truthfulness. Tanaka was testing Haverkamp to see if he lived up to the standards of Christian truthfulness he is supposed to profess. If he had lied, Tanaka would have felt justified in punishing him severely. Haverkamp, to him, would have been a most dishonest man, guilty of a breach of camp discipline and dishonourable by his own professed code to boot. What happened to the rice?"

Van Reebek raised his eyebrows. The question was unexpected.

"I will find out, Kapitan."

"Because that was a more cruel blow than a beating. Having traded his boots for it, Haverkamp still has an empty belly and will have to work to the end of time barefooted."

"It was a good thing, Kapitan, that Timmers was also not searched."

"Oh. Why? What has our fat friend been up to now?"

"Only brought in a whole chicken, Kapitan."

The Commandant tried to purse his lips to whistle.

"In his loin-cloth?"

"As you say. In his loin-cloth. The bird was asleep in a bush by that kampong just beside the airstrip. Timmers was working at a place near there. When he first showed it to me its head was still under its wing, but the neck was cut right through. He took off the feathers, cut it in pieces and brought it in between his legs."

The Commandant gave a grunt that might have been a laugh.

"Your people in Java convicted Timmers as a homicidal lunatic. Like so many other things, lunacy appears to be relative. Has he made any more knives lately?"

"I heard them say in my barracks as I ate my 'pap' that it was just to try a new one that he killed the chicken."

"Is there anything to show that he is planning to stick it into someone?"

"Since you saved him from being beaten to death by the Yap sergeant after he had tried to kill DeBoers, Kapitan, he has been quiet, reasonable and friendly. He is always coming to me to tell me what a good Commandant you are. Maar . . ." Van Reebek shrugged. "Is there anything to show? It is impossible to find out. I have two men watching him all the time. They have his confidence and sleep next to him, one on each side."

"They are brave men."

Van Reebek shook his head.

"They will share his chicken tonight. He is a good provider and generous to his freiends."

"And to himself. The only two men in the camp who can still boast of having bellies are Jansen down at the cookhouse and Timmers."

"That Jansen, Kapitan. Can't you take him from being chief cook?"

"Unfortunately, no. His appointment comes from the Japanese. He has a pull somewhere with the guard and the Sergeant. I think I know what it is, but until I'm sure I can't do anything."

"When will you be sure, Kapitan?"

"That he passes information to the Japs?"

"Oh! So he is the one?"

"There are others."

"A white man who will inform against his own people for a little extra food!" Then Van Reebek blushed, remembering that he wasn't really a white man himself. He changed the subject.

"I brought a paper, Kapitan." He took a small, well-folded piece of paper out of the top pocket of his worn tunic. It was a foolscap sheet closely covered with type. It was in English— a newspaper published by the Japanese for the educated Malays and Chinese.

If Van Reebek had been caught at the guard post as he brought it in he might have been killed.

"Well done. Is there anything new in it?"

"It seems as if there have been landings in Mindoro, as the Yaponser claim to have won a great victory there."

"If they run true to form, that is probably the first and last we shall hear of that island."

Van Reebek went on:

"On the west front it is much like last week."

He handed the paper over.

"I'll read it later. Thank you. You had better go and sleep. Are you going out again tonight?"

"Yes, Kapitan."

"You are a good fellow, Van Reebek. You do a good job."

As Van Reebek walked away, two emotions fought within him.

He did not like the British, he never had. In Singapore and elsewhere they had clubs where people like himself were forbidden entry. At the same time, this Britisher entrusted him with difficult jobs and spoke with him as an equal.

What was he to think of him? He would have liked to believe in him and respect him, but . . . it was impossible to tell whether such a man might not slam the door in his face should he be found out to be a half-caste. The young Dutchman shrugged again and shook his head.

Ten minutes later he was asleep on his plank bed in the officers' billet.

CHAPTER II

THE Commandant, his mind heavy with an inertia that was daily spreading up to obscure his intelligence, as a cataract obscures the sight of an eye, was lying propped against the wall at his back, staring at the cracked red-wood boards above the dingy cotton blanket and the cropped head of the man on the sleeping bench opposite to him.

Then Doctor DeGoyer came in through the door on the Commandant's right and blocked his line of vision.

Without a word the doctor took a grip of one of the Commandant's swollen ankles and dug his fingers into it as hard as he could. He continued to grip it like that for more than half a minute. When he took his hand away he left five pits each half an inch deep in the puffed flesh.

"Like prodding a piece of dough," said the Commandant.

Doctor DeGoyer smiled. It was the famous smile with the light behind the eyes which gave his hungry, frog-like features a puckish twist, a smile that had brought to his door most of the wealthy women of Amsterdam in the days before a German invasion had seemed imminent and the Doctor had left his rich practice there to do a little "field-work" in Java.

"Ya, as you say, a piece of dough. And how goes it today, Kapitan?"

"I feel fine, thank you, DeGoyer." The Commandant found that with an effort of will he could shake his mind clear of its apathy. The pricking of the antagonism he felt for the professional grin in front of him helped him.

"Then that is all that is important. Feel fine and you vill be fine. Feel . . . how do you say it . . . lousy, and you will be lousy. Niet?"

The smile was gone, then reappeared for the next patient as the Doctor paced on down the hut.

Watching DeGoyer move from patient to patient, the Commandant was reminded of an old-fashioned actor crossing a stage and bowing his thanks to the thin applause that comes from a bored audience.

"Charlatan." The Commandant actually mouthed the word, though no sound came from his lips. It was a symptom of his illness that he became easily upset, lifting quickly from lethargy to shaking fury.

Before he became seriously ill he had been able to ignore his dislike for DeGoyer. Now, though he could suppress any outward show of his feelings when he was face to face with the man, the fire of indignation that was lit in him had to burn right up before it could be quenched.

What made the Commandant more angry than anything else was the awareness that DeGoyer was the most successful doctor in the camp.

The Commandant knew him to be a confidence trickster, as shallow and insincere as an auction tout at a sale. Yet the man had the ability to sell to his patients the belief that he was a brilliant doctor and able to cure them. In a prison camp, where there were few drugs available, it placed him in a winning position over the other doctors, who still tried to work scientifically.

The man had another evil characteristic. He was too easily corruptible. Where the morality of a community was so dependent upon the example set by its leaders, the Commandant found it tragic that one of them, who was always in the limelight, was capable of selling his professional services for some of his patients' already inadequate food. The man was criminally iniquitous, and the Commandant was powerless to correct him, because he did succeed in keeping men alive who might otherwise have died, and also because if he was forbidden to practise he would be driven over to the other side and would prove a useful recruit to the small opposition to authority and discipline which existed in the camp. To have appealed to any sense of honour in the man would have been a bad joke, for he knew honour only as something that could be used as a theatrical gesture.

Presently the Commandant felt his indignation draining away. For a moment it had filled him with an angry vitality. But he had to acknowledge that there was nothing he could do about the Doctor's behaviour, that his rage was futile. It pumped him up and left him as flat and limp afterwards as a balloon that has been let down.

With relief he saw Doctor Bruin come into the barrack. He was the Senior Medical Officer in the camp and the Commandant's only intimate friend. He was a young man, younger that DeGoyer but senior to him in army rank, having been in the Dutch Army Medical Reserve ever since he had first qualified.

The Commandant watched him as he stood and talked with Schiller, the young orderly in charge of the barrack. The man who had died in the night had to be buried and his few effects disposed of. It was almost a daily task for Schiller, and Doctor Bruin did not have to spend long with him giving him his instructions.

Soon he came on up the narrow gangway towards the Commandant's bed-space. He was tall and fair, with a brusque, direct manner that seemed to be natural to him until he came close enough for an observer to notice the expression of his eyes. Behind light-rimmed spectacles they were blue and still —after so long as a prisoner of war—inclined to crinkle quickly into an expression of almost insolent humour.

He spoke natural, easy English, had studied in England for a few years before the war, and had been as valuable to the Commandant as sight itself during the long years that they had spent together.

"Well, Huth, how are you this morning?" The Doctor sat himself at the Commandant's feet.

"I'm just getting over DeGoyer's morning visit."

Bruin smiled, glanced along the hut towards his fellow doctor and then down at the dents in the Commandant's bare ankles.

"So I see," he said. Reaching forward, he took the Commandant's pulse and watched the laboured rise and fall of his chest. Behind his unconcerned expression, Bruin was unhappy. He had seen this old man's value from the beginning and had nursed him, fostering him like a mother with a brilliant child, protecting him as far as he could from unnecessary, petty responsibilities and then throwing the full weight of his authority behind those major decisions and rulings which the Commandant made with such well-judged authority when they were necessary. He spent a lot of time, too, interpreting the Britisher to the Dutch in the camp. He acknowledged unreservedly the honesty and dependability of the older man's wisdom and judgment and. with a certain reserve, returned the affection that he knew the Commandant had for him. This element of reserve was not due to any flaw in their relationship but to a private problem which Bruin preferred not to discuss with anyone. The Commandant on his side sensed the reserve and accepted it without curiosity, satisfied to have beside him a man whom he could respect and trust.

But now Bruin could see that the Commandant was slipping away from him and that the pace of his descent was growing daily faster, and he felt as if the ground beneath his feet was becoming uncertain. Some time soon he would have to step back on to firmer soil, to withdraw the contact that he knew meant much to both of them, for fear that the Commandant's fall might bring him down too. Bruin knew that he still had much strength to give to those who were weaker than himself and that it would not be right to forfeit that strength out of any sentimental feelings which he had for the dying man. Later this problem was to become more acute . . . but even for the present, that he saw what lay ahead of him was enough to make him examine his defences.

Looking now at the man that beriberi had turned into a grotesque bladder of moist tissue, Bruin thought again of him as he had seen him first in a camp in Java, a small, lean, wiry man, most neatly put together. His hair and moustache, now almost pure white, were even then past the stage of being grey, and his eyes, which were too pale a shade of blue to be a good feature, were set in a splintering of fine wrinkles that stretched out towards his high cheek-bones—eyes which now looked as if they had been painted on a surface of distended rubber.

Coming back to the present with a jerk, Bruin asked:

"Breathing more difficult?"

"I suppose it is. I have a feeling that if I forget about it, it might stop."

Bruin nodded. "Well, don't let it dismay you too much. The automatic nervous system will still carry on working the bellows for quite a long time yet, and then as soon as the sergeant gets me some injections of Vitamin B1, you will be on your feet again in ten days."

The Commandant shook his head slightly.

"If you get some B1 you will have to give it to youngsters like Wim Peterson over there," he said, "not to old dodderers like me."

Bruin's eyes crinkled and he too shook his head.

"What I do with the B1 is my business, not yours. Besides, we may be lucky and get enough for everyone." And then, before the Commandant could speak again, he went on:

"But I didn't come here to discuss how we are going to treat your beriberi, I came to give you a problem to chew over. It is something which as Commandant of the camp you are going to have to decide for us."

The Commandant felt like telling the Doctor to take his problems to hell. Then he realised that Bruin was bringing it to him so that he should have something to stimulate his mind and carry him over his inertia. Pleased to have seen through the Doctor's ruse, he said quite eagerly:

"All right. What is it?"

"Tobacco," said Bruin. "Yoshimitsu sent for me last night and said that he could get us half a ton of native tobacco if we could find the money in the camp to pay for it. Of course, the money won't be difficult . . . the price isn't very great and the smokers will all put in their last cent for something to smoke." He paused.

"So?" asked the Commandant. "What is the problem?"

"Should we buy it?"

"Why not?"

"For two reasons. The first, not really a concern of ours perhaps: there may be a chance later to buy food. The money would be better spent that way. Secondly, nicotine poisoning kills the nerve endings . . . it has the same effect as beriberi, particularly dry beriberi. . . . I am afraid it will probably hasten the development of the disease in those who are still only suffering with it in a slight form. It may kill them much more quickly than they would die normally, if they didn't have the tobacco. At the same time, there can be no doubt of the benefit most of those cases get on the side of morale. It is tremendous, perhaps enough to pull some of them round. What do we do? No, don't answer quickly, think about it and tell me what you decide. All right?"

"It doesn't seem to be a very difficult problem," said the Commandant, "but if you insist, I'll think about it."

He sat up slowly and with difficulty, breathing harder all the time, and started to delve under the small pile of clothes he used for a pillow. After a moment he brought out a thick exercise book with a shiny black cover. He handed it to Doctor Bruin.

"And since I'm going to do something for you, Jan . . . perhaps you'll do something for me."

"Ah!" said Bruin, and his eyes held their expression of banter again. "THE book."

"Yes, THE book. I've long promised you that you should read it. Well, take it now and do that very thing."

Bruin took it, turning it in his hands. As the Commandant had known that Bruin was giving him a problem to stimulate him and help to keep him alive, so, now, Bruin knew that the book was not just being given to him to read, but for safe keeping.

He forced the impudent look and tone again, and said lightly, "I'll guard it as if it were my own 'apology to the world for not having done better' . . . and I'll read it and return it."

The Commandant lay back with a sigh. He felt relieved. "Yes," he said, "do that. Go away and read it and then bring it back. In the meantime, I'll give my most serious consideration to the problem of tobacco." And suddenly he laughed. "Jan, you are a rascal," he said. "Come again soon and stay longer next time."

2

From between the tall, pale trunks of the rubber trees the sun was drawing the moisture of a recent shower back towards the tree-tops, where it formed a thick mist, and the tree boles shone against the dark shadows that the foliage and mist cast across the ground. In the occasional rays of sunlight that struck right through to the stamped-down mud surrounds of the camp it was possible to see the vapour rising like smoke from a camp fire on a still day.

Though it was mid-morning it was hard to believe that the camp contained any life at all. The ramshackle huts with rusty galvanised tin roofs stood silent and apparently empty. Through the big, square, casementless windows, with single galvanised iron shutters hinged at the top and propped open at the bottom with long poles, it was possible to see into the dark interiors of the huts. And there too was no movement. In the hospital barrack the heat lay like a thick, steamy towel across all its occupants, making even those who were delirious supine and limp.

In the other barracks the night shift slept the dead sleep of exhaustion while their companions across the water laboured, sweating and cursing in the sun, as they carted baskets full of earth to build blast walls round aircraft dispersal bays.

Schiller, who was the only trained male nurse in the camp, seemed also to be the only man moving anywhere on the island. He was returning from emptying two buckets that were used as earth closets by the most feeble of the dysentery cases. As he passed a somnolent Korean sentry at the guard point on the camp's perimeter, he put the buckets down, turned and faced the sentry and then bowed stiffly to him from the hips. The sentry inclined his head slightly, acknowledging the salute. Schiller picked his buckets up again and proceeded on his way. He had had to make the same obeisance going to the bog as he had returning, and to the same guard post. On an earlier occasion he had bowed without setting the buckets down. The guard had promptly slapped his face for insulting the Emperor of Japan's uniform by saluting with a bucket of excreta in his hand.

Schiller returned to the barrack. He set the buckets down, covered them with wooden lids, went and washed his hands and then, filling another bucket with clean water, he walked with it down the narrow gangway to the Commandant's bed place.

Every day Schiller gave the Commandant a bath. It was a duty he performed for the old man alone of all the patients.

He was a young man of twenty-three, a homosexual who had taken to male nursing because it offered him an outlet for the feminine need to care for people he felt in himself. Three years of prison-camp diet had quenched in him, as it had quenched in all the other normal prisoners, most of the sex urge, and it had left Schiller, drained of his inverted instincts, with only his compassion for those who were suffering and with a great desire to help them in their need for sympathy and attention.

Since he had first joined the Commandant's draft of prisoners in Java, the young man had had a fixation for his British commander. In it there still lingered an element of his abnormal sexual instincts. Schiller, when properly nourished, had had the fleshiness, the narrow shoulders and the broad hips typical of his twisted nature. In the Commandant's hard virility and natural air of authority he found the complement of his own soft womanliness.

The Commandant, sensing the younger man's devotion, but not being aware of its origin, helped to increase Schiller's passion by going out of his way to be kind to him, in a distant but fatherly way.

Bruin, who knew more about Schiller than the Commandant and quite deliberately used to its maximum the young man's gifts for nursing, was cynically amused by the Commandant's blindness and didn't trouble to explain the situation to him, as he believed, rightly, that the old man would have been made uncomfortable if he had known the true facts of the case.

In an uncertain way the Commandant did sense that there was something odd in Schiller's manner as he served him, but he never felt the need to analyse his faint mistrust. If there was a dark side to Schiller's devotion it was more than compensated for, in the Commandant's eyes, by the young man's endlessly unselfish work for the sick who lay heaped together along the shelves on each side of the hut.

There had been one occasion, earlier, when Schiller had bathed him after a bout of fever, when the Commandant had been faintly aware that the boy's approach to him had something abnormal in it, but the realisation had come through the veil of exquisite relaxation that follows the final break in a high fever and was part of a dream that was not altogether to be credited by the waking senses.

Poor Schiller, now that he had his idol helplessly in his power and dependent upon him for everything, was happy in his upside-down heart at one moment, and acutely miserable at the next, for even he could not blind himself to the speed with which the old man had been failing for the last few days.

"Will you take your bath now, Kapitan?" he asked as he came up to the Commandant's bed space. The Commandant wanted to smile. There was always this pretence of allowing him to decide whether he should be bathed, whether he was ready for his rice 'pap' in the morning, or his rice and potato-stew at lunch-time, or his rice 'pap' for supper.

Carefully, he replied, as he always did, "Yes, I think it would be convenient now, Schiller, thank you."

Schiller rigged a mat up as a screen on the open side of the Commandant's bed space. At the same time the Commandant turned so that his head was to the gangway and his feet to the wall. Schiller started to wash his face, neck and shoulders.

The young man's touch was as gentle as a mother's.

Presently he said, "Kapitan, I prayed to God last night that the Yap sergeant would bring in much B1. And I asked that if it was impossible for him to get a lot . . . then that he would bring in enough for Doctor Bruin to treat you."

"That was very kind of you, Schiller."

But the Commandant felt uneasy. Schiller was an eager Catholic. The Commandant was an impatient atheist, impatient, that is, with others who were not atheists. At the same time, and with an effort which became greater every day as his sickness increased, he made an endeavour to control his impatience, for he knew that if he were drawn into argument and destroyed another's faith he would, under the circumstances prevailing in a prison camp, be guilty of murder.

"Now you must pray to God too, Kapitan." The Commandant sat up so that Schiller could wash his back. "Then he will make you well again."

There was a pause. With his back rinsed and dried the Commandant turned again and lay down with his feet towards Schiller. With soft, soapy hands the boy continued with his washing.

"There are many people praying for you, Kapitan. Father Van Fleet has told all of us to say special novenas for you. And our prayers will be answered. You know that, don't you?"

The Commandant closed his eyes, willing himself to be silent. When he opened them again he found them filled with a sudden blurred brilliance, a shining thistle of light. For a second he wondered if he was about to be visited by an apparition, perhaps St. Peter. Then he saw that the sun was striking straight into his eyes through a chink in the corrugated iron roof.

He turned his head irritably so that he was not looking at the light any more.

"Who was the man who died last night?" he asked.

"That was DenVelde, Kapitan."

The Commandant hunted for a face to fit the name of DenVelde, but could not find one.

"I don't remember him," he said.

"He is at rest with the Father in Heaven now," said Schiller, his hands busy with a towel. When he had rubbed the Commandent's skin dry he turned him on his face. Somewhere Schiller had found a small bottle of methylated spirit. It should have been kept for more important uses, but he insisted on rubbing the Commandant's buttocks with it. As he rubbed he said:

"Jesus Christ suffered for other people as you have suffered, Kapitan. God will reward you as He rewarded His Son." The Commandant had his eyes shut again. Without opening them, he said:

"I believe those well-meant words might be sacrilegious. You'd better confess to the Reverend Father and don't make such statements again, or you may burn in hell-fire for them . . . and I'm not worth that."

When, after two or three seconds, there was no reply, the Commandant opened his eyes and looked backwards over his shoulder.

Schiller was standing to attention at the side of the bed-space. In front of him and looking down on the naked back view of the Commandant was a Korean soldier.

The Commandant turned over and struggled rather laboriously to get into his sarong. The Korean indicated that the orderly should help.

When the Commandant was covered from the waist downwards, the Korean sat on the edge of the bed, and waved Schiller away.

Stumblingly, in bad Malay, he enquired after the Commandant's health. His words were no mere formality; there was genuine concern in his tone.

The Commandant took the enquiry as it was meant and replied that he didn't really think that he was much better.

The Korean shook his head sadly and produced three words of English.

"War no good," he said and, relapsing back into Malay, continued a tale that he had repeated often before. It was about how he had not seen his family for five years; how happy he had been on his farm just north of the Korean capital; how he hoped to go back and work his fields again and live with his wife and children. And again he shook his head and said:

"War no good."

Then he suddenly changed his expression. Haltingly, he produced some more English.

"After tomorrow"—he waved his hands in a gesture to denote something a bit further away than the immediate present —"Chrissy . . . maas."

The Commandant said, "The day after tomorrow is Christmas Day. Yes."

The Korean nodded enthusiastically, smiling.

"Present," he said. "I . . . give . . . you . . . Chrissy . . . maas present."

And he brought out of his pocket two packets of Japanese KOOA cigarettes.

For a long moment the Commandant was tongue-tied. He had no right to accept cigarettes, though the sight of them made him hunger frantically for the taste of good tobacco.

He looked at his would-be benefactor's smooth, hairless, yellow face and it was alive with goodwill and childishly vulnerable to rebuff.

He sighed and took the cigarettes.

"Thank you," he said. The Korean got up, still smiling and held out his hand.

"Happy Chrissy . . . maas."

With a feeling of sickness the Commandant took the proffered hand.

"Happy Christmas," he replied. They then sketched a bow to each other and the Korean left.

For a long time the Commandant sat looking at the two packets of cigarettes. They were wrapped as American cigarettes are, in a neat, closely pressed block. The wrapping papers with their large letterings were as new and clean as they were when they had come out of the carton.

"New and clean." The Commandant wondered how long it was since he had seen anything which was new and clean. Everything in the camp was so very second-hand and worn out. The people along with their possessions and their ideas. There was nothing new—only these two packets of cigarettes.

Schiller had been hovering in the distance ever since the Korean had left the barrack. The Commandant called him and handed him a packet. He had meant to hand him both packets, but at the last moment he found that the gesture was going to cost him too much. The only new thing in the camp . . . and good tobacco.

"Thank you, Kapitan, I don't smoke," said Schiller, handing the packet back.

"Take them, damn you," said the Commandant, forcing them into his hand again, "and don't argue. You can find somebody who does smoke to give them to more easily than I can."

"But they are a present from a Yap."

The Commandant was shaking with anger. With a quick gesture he slapped the packet out of the boy's hand. It fell on the dirt floor.

Schiller, with a surprised look, bent and picked it up. The paper wrapper was soiled.

The Commandant couldn't trust himself to speak. He felt a lump rise in his throat, felt again as he had felt when as a child he had been wrongfully punished, fighting between hurt and anger.

At last he said, "Oh, go away, go away."

Schiller looked miserable and puzzled, but he left.

Slowly the Commandant undid his packet, carefully slitting the side of it so that the gummed edges came apart. Then he spread the paper out flat on the board plank beside him.

Still gazing at it, he turned the wheel of his lighter on the flint . . . gently blew the slow match to a glow and lit himself a cigarette.

3

Timmers was beating the bottom of his aluminium food dish with his spoon.

The hut in which he stood was built on a steep slope. At the end which was highest up the slope the two bedding shelves were only a foot off the ground, but they ran out horizontally for the length of the hut so that at the other end, some fifty feet away, they stood eight feet above the ground and the occupants at that end had to use ladders to climb up to their and two opposite to each other halfway down its narrow bed-spaces. There was a door at the uphill end of the hut length.

The hut was occupied entirely by Indonesians and half-castes, men who were used to living in the tropics and who knew that the way to keep a building cool was to create a draught through it by closing the corrugated iron shutters, leaving only one partly open at the doorless end to balance the open door up the hill. Thus the sun was excluded and the little wind tempted into the hut was forced through its whole length before it could find an outlet.

Timmers had his bed-space at the highest part of the bedding shelf and nearest to the window that was kept open. So he had the coolest place in the hut and one which was placed, during the hours of daylight, in a most dramatic light.

He was standing in this light now and against the rattling of his spoon was announcing the song he was going to sing that evening. He was a smiling little man, plump and the colour of milk chocolate. Except for his head and the upper corners of his mouth, his skin was hairless. In his ancestry there was Javanese, Chinese and Dutch blood. From the second of these lines of predecessors he had inherited narrow, elliptical eyes and a thin sprouting of moustaches which fell past his fat, beardless cheeks and down each side of his full, beautiful Javanese mouth. His sly but not unamiable eyes were as black as his moustaches. His hands were unnaturally small, as were his feet, and his fingernails, which were so pale in colour that they seemed to tip his fingers with peeled almonds, were fragile and of a lovely shape.

Timmers had been found by a Dutch court in Java to be a homicidal lunatic, after a series of mysterious killings had emptied a large kampong near Sourabaja of all save its bravest inhabitants. It had never been conclusively proved that all the twenty-eight persons who had been found scientifically knifed had been murdered by Timmers. But, from the neatness of the execution in each case, the judge had felt that it was almost a matter of a trade-mark and had assumed the guilt to have been Timmers'.

When the Japanese had needed more men for their forced labour camps, Timmers, along with the rest of the contents of his jail, had been amnestied, taken from behind stone walls and placed behind barbed wire. Shortly afterwards he had been shipped from Java to the island on which he was now held as a prisoner of war among other prisoners of war.

There could be no doubt that he was homicidal and evidence could be found to prove that his mind had softened in other ways as well. To make up, however, for these soft patches, there were parts of his brain which were uncommonly hard. Handled with understanding, he could usually be depended upon to behave quite well, if with a sly tendency to be self-seeking. But just occasionally his balance went like a run-down top. When this occurred his plump, soft little body became consumed with a slow-burning, feverish heat that built itself up and up until his blood could only be cooled by letting the blood of another.

So far as was known, during the last two years he had killed only one man. His victim had been an unfortunate Malayan coolie on the airfield who had angered Timmers by trying to diddle the little man over a deal in illicit rice.

The only other occasion when he had run amok was the one that Van Reebek had mentioned that morning to the Commandant.

Timmers had, as had many of his people, a gift for making extempore verse which was fitted to one of several traditional folk tunes. He had commemorated the occasion when he had run amok with a long piece of heroic poetry.

Since composing it he had never written a word of its many verses on paper, but could without effort repeat it word for word as he had first conceived it. However, like all artists, he could never agree that any composition he made was perfect: so that there was a chance that at each repetition some part might be changed to suit his mood of the moment or because, in its original form, it did not achieve the heights of artistry that were his goal.

Every evening before going out with the night shift he treated the hut to one of his compositions. His "Amok" poem was his favourite, but there were many others. In one which dealt with the death of twenty-seven men in a Kampong near Sourabaja there were some verses which complained about a miscarriage of justice because he had been convicted of twenty-eight murders. The poem went on to explain that someone must have sheltered under the cloak of his killings to pay off a private score.

Practically all his listeners knew his verses by heart and would emphasise the most lurid parts by joining in with him as he sang.

This evening he had announced an hour earlier that it was to be the "Amok" poem. He was giving it because he had heard that the Commandant was seriously ill and he wished to do his one-time benefactor this honour in the hope that it would help him in recovery.

Van Reebek, who was in charge of the barrack, had heard that it was to be the "Amok" poem and had come along to make a transcription of it in English, so that Timmers could present it to the Commandant as a Christmas present.

As always when the little half-caste beat his dixie, he got silence immediately. Those who didn't want to hear his song, and they made up nearly eighty per cent of the hut's complement, had already left and were sitting outside in the gathering dusk. Timmers' followers, though in the minority, were fanatically devoted to the little man's songs and would brook no disturbance during a performance.

Timmers waited a full minute to be sure that everyone was attentive before he began.

Van Reebek already knew the song by heart and was in attendance only to check what he had written.

Timmers then sang.

"Many white men, many white men"—Timmers adopted the tone of a priest declaiming a descant, which suited the poem admirably, as its wording showed the influence of the Bible, upon which he had been brought up in his childhood—"men with white skins, are soft like the roots of the jungle fern. My knives are sharp and can kill such men as easily as they can cut the fern roots.

"There are several of these white-root men here in the camp. Among them there is one who is even worse than the rest. He is a bad man, a man who steals and lies. He is a man who does not live his life straight, but lives it twistedly like the snake fish on the bed of the sea.

"This white man steals the dreams of the black men. He walks in the night and steals their dreams. He is jealous of them because they are still men and can lie in bed and think with pleasure of their women.

"The white-root man would steal the black men's women though he cannot use them. He was planning to steal my woman. So I took one of my little shining friends that I sleep with every night and I went to seek the white-root man.

"I went to his hall and I called to him. I called, 'Come out, white-root man, come out. I have a friend here I want you to meet. She is cool and beautiful and I sleep with her every night.'

"Then the white-root man came to me in the evening light. Came eagerly because he thought he could take one of my women. But as he came he brought others to share the delights, tho' none had the power left to lay with a woman as a man should lay with her.

"Then came also the yellow men of the guard. And they

held me and took away my cool beautiful one. And they led me into a hole in the ground which they closed on me so that I saw no more the light of the sun.

"In that darkness voices whispered to me. They came from the planks in the floor, the timbers of the wall and from the roof beams. And they said, 'Here you will die. Here we shall take the breath from your nostrils and block all the passages which enter and leave your body and you will die there within yourself.'

"And the darkness was full of other things . . . that crept slimily over my belly and salt blood that dripped from the roof on my lips. I cried, alone there in the darkness, and was full of fear and my bowels gave up their content, so that I lay in it and was foul.

"Through the darkness I called for help, calling, calling, for I was a man undone by his enemies. The white-root man had undone me and given me to the saffron devils for them to beat and torture.

"Then came the one with the blue sky behind his eyes, the little one with the white head, the man who knows all men to be his brothers: for whom there is no black and no white: the man who is black to the blacks and white to the whites.

"He came and he stood before me and ordered me to wash, saying that he was to come with me to the yellow turds to stand by my side. But he said, 'Wash, for I will not stand beside you while you are foul.' Then I washed and went with him.

"And we came to the slender one with the black hair who is a saffron brother to the devil. This one said to me, 'My men tell me you are one who likes to use knives . . . take a knife, then, for I too am one who likes to use knives.'

"Then he gave me a knife and stood before me and prodded my belly with the point of his long knife so that there were beads of blood upon it.

"And the one with the sky behind his eyes stood beside me and said to me, 'Keep the point of your knife down to the earth. Do not fight with this man, for he used a sword to cut the knot of his mother's teat so that he might have suck!'

"And the yellow one touched me here and there; he touched me everywhere, and everywhere there came beads of blood. Then the one who stood beside me cried 'Enough, Yoshimitsu, enough. Your sword is sharper than your intelligence . . . for this man you are punishing is no evil doer, no child to be taught with hard words and pain. He is but a man formed in another cast to ourselves.'

"And Yoshimitsu replied, 'He is evil. His form is as ours is, but it is possessed of evil. The only way to be rid of it is to drive it out by fear with the whip and the sword.'

"Then said my protector, 'Try my way first.' And the other replied, 'We have tried your way and it failed. But as he will not take the sword which he professed to love, then we shall beat him.'

"'Then you must beat me too, for in my country we learned two hundred years ago that the whip would not drive out the sickness that this one suffers from . . . and I am as guilty as he, for before my own God I swore that I would never let him have the opportunity to get sick again.'

"Silent. The yellow man was silent and the point of his sword hung to the ground. At last he said, 'You shall come with me and stand with this man, for I will beat him, but only a little and you shall tell me when to stop.'

"Then through the half light, for it was near evening time, they took me to the '*midqn*', there beyond the huts, and I was tied to a tree and there I was left, alone, save for my protector, who spoke kindly to me, for the time it took the yellow one to eat his rice.

"When he came back he brought with him all the men of the camp. There in the darkness they stood round. Aye, you my brothers stood round. In your hands you held oil wicks and I stood looking at you and you were all moons and flickering stars come to watch my degradation.

"Yoshimitsu bore with him a thin bamboo. And he stood before me, with his back before me, and though I knew great fear, I knew too that had I one of my silver sisters with me and my hands free he would have died there.

"Then he made a loud voice and called to you saying, 'See, this one is evil, he would have killed one of his own sort.' But the white-root men are not my sort—all save the one who stood there constantly by my side.

"In the darkness, you my brothers held fireflies and your faces floated like moons above them. Thus was I ringed with fireflies, bank upon bank of them lighting my degradation.

"Only the Constant One was there beside me. Then turned Yoshimitsu and tore my loin-cloth from me and I stood before

34

you, ashamed, with my man parts hanging down before me for all to see.

"And the same made me shiver like I was cold, for I was so truly ashamed. Then Yoshimitsu sliced me about the legs and thighs with the bamboo and made sport with my man parts saying he would cut them off.

"And the shame: the shame of being made to reveal myself to all men—white-root men and black men who were gathered there.

"Then the Constant One stopped the saffron turd quickly saying, 'Enough. Now you must beat me.' And the yellow one said, 'If you say it is enough, then I hear you. But this man must stay here tied to the tree until dawn. Perhaps the spirit is frightened enough now to wish to escape away in the dark.'

"When Yoshimitsu went away, then the one with the sky behind his eyes took a small cloth from his pocket and covered me, hanging it before me so that I need not spend the night in shame, for . . ."

Van Reebek looked at his watch. He had most of the story correct and he had to report to the Commandant before he took his working party away. He had only just time for that. He left the barrack quickly and crossed to the one in which the Commandant lay.

In the light of a hurricane lamp the old man was lying on his back and though his eyes were open it seemed as if he slept.

Van Reebek saluted silently, took a deep breath, wished he could shift the load of responsibility that lay ahead in the evening's work and then turned and forced himself to step out again into the night with a convincing pretence of confidence and purpose.

CHAPTER III

SMITH was playing a game with his Bible; though he would never have acknowledged that it was a game. He knew that instead of treating the Holy Word as a lottery it would be more likely to earn him Grace if he read it through from cover to cover. But that would require concentration. What Smith had to have was a pastime.

When it occurred to him that his game might be frowned upon by the Elders of his Church, he told himself that nothing he did which might lead to his knowing the word of God better could really be a weakness or a wickedness.

His game was a simple one.

Having decided on the Old or the New Testament, he thought of a page number. Then he started reading at the first chapter heading on that page, or on the next one if the text on the page he had chosen was unbroken by chapter headings. At the second cross-reference-index he would turn away from the chapter and find the reference. He would read on from there to the next second cross-reference: which he would look up and read on again from there and so on, continuing to turn away at each second cross-reference until the game palled.

This evening is was the Old Testament and the page number he chose was seven hundred and forty-five. On that page he found Chapter Four of Ecclesiastes.

He began to read:

"So I returned and considered the oppressions that are done under the sun: and behold the tears of such as were oppressed, and they had no comforter; and on the side of their oppressors there was power; and they had no comforter.

"Wherefore I praised the dead which are already dead more than the living which are yet alive. Yea better is he than both they, which hath not yet been, who hath not seen the evil work that is done under the sun."

At the beginning of the last verse was a small letter "b" indicating the cross-reference. It was to Job. 3. 11.

He turned back and read:

"Why died I not from the womb? Why did I not give up the ghost when I came out of the belly?

"Why did the knees prevent me? or why the breasts that I should suck?

"For now should I have lain still and been quiet, I should have slept: then had I been at rest."

Smith knew both quotations by heart.

He had found them one day some weeks earlier, and his will was too feeble to resist the temptation to come back on them.

Unfortunately too, his weakness in returning so regularly to page seven hundred and forty-five defeated the object of his game. He could not get past the words "then had I been at rest."

Physically he had nothing to do but lie and rest all day. Spiritually, he was living in a delirium. With restless uncertainty, the soul he had dedicated to God turned miserably backwards and forwards within him. Only oblivion could still it.

Smith had found that with practice oblivion could be commanded at will.

He sighed, relaxed and dropped his head back on the small pile of clothes that was his pillow. His mind went blank. Sometimes for minutes together he was able to keep it blank.

Today the first returning consciousness came through his fingertips. What he felt was the cool smoothness of the laced thongs of bamboo that went to make up the mat he was lying on. Through the sense of touch he was brought back to the world of realities and he returned to it gladly, forcing himself up into a sitting position. His surroundings gave him little enough to grasp, in this world a bare finger-hold. His room was a cell, seven feet wide and ten feet long. The walls were of smoky, untreated mahogany, pierced by two small barred windows and a doorway without a door.

Smith sat on a bench that ran the length of the room and was a foot narrower than the room's width. Before him, along the wall in which the door occupied the further end from him, was the gangway that enabled him to get to his sleeping mat without walking over the other two bed spaces which paralleled his.

Doctor Bruin and the Commandant had originally shared his narrow quarters, but the Commandant, at his own request, had been moved to the hospital barrack: so Smith was alone now with Doctor Bruin.

"Three little nigger boys playing with some glue
One got stuck and then there were two."

Smith shook his head. Those were not the right words, but it didn't matter.

Immediately his mind told him, for the thousandth time, what did matter. It was that he had no responsibility to anyone except God, and he was failing to fulfil that responsibility.

He was failing God, his Captain.

It was a realisation that he had not been able to escape from for months.

Still, he consoled himself, there was a refuge ahead: the day after tomorrow was Christmas Day.

The Japanese had forbidden church services in their prison camps, but he, Smith, had gone with Doctor Bruin to ask the Japanese for permission to hold a Christmas service. They had, in fact, asked permission for three services, one for the Catholics, one for the Protestants and one for the Nonconformists.

When they went to him, Yoshimitsu had sat silently for a long time considering their request.

Smith had watched him. The Sergeant's slight, tense figure gave off, even in stillness, a radiant energy. But Smith had failed to see, as he had always failed to see, beyond the physical characteristics of the man. To Smith all men with slanting eyes and yellow skins looked the same. They were worse than foreigners, they were a different species altogether. The Bible said that God made all men in His Own Image. In Smith's mind that image was for ever associated with the figure of a tall, pale man with a fanatic's glowing eyes and a long, golden beard of soft lustrous hair. It was possible to convert others to the same belief. Smith had done it among the black men in West Africa, but the image he expected them to reverence remained the same. Before the Japanese had made him shave his head, it was an image that Smith could associate in some way with himself, so that a little of the worship spilled over at his own feet.

Presently the Sergeant had asked:

"Do all these religions worship the same God?"

Smith had not seen the trap.

38

"Yes," he had replied. He hadn't even had the sense to say, "Yes, but in a different way."

"Good," said Yoshimitsu. "You have one God, you may have one service." And he had turned his back on them.

Smith had not appreciated the subleties that had prompted the Sergeant's answer. He took it as another insult and one, like all the others, that had to be borne.

Yoshimitsu had not intended any insult at all. To him his answer had seemed logical and at the same time one which followed the rule that required him never to appear to give anything away free. Discipline would be sure to suffer if the prisoners came to believe that they had only to ask and everything they asked for would be given them.

There was no appeal beyond Yoshimitsu.

Since only one service was to be permitted, it was arranged so that all the sects could attend it without injury to their principles. Smith had been surprised how readily the other priests in the camp, though Dutch, had co-operated.

Smith's part in the service, as he spoke no Dutch, was to read the second lesson in English.

He picked up his Bible again and finding the place started to read aloud, but softly, from the middle of the Christmas lesson.

"And suddenly there was with the angel a multitude of the heavenly host praising God and saying:

"Glory to God in the highest and on earth peace, goodwill toward men . . ."

The words flowed over Smith in a warm, comforting stream. He sat back and read on, silently now, and absorbed.

2

A little way off, outside the hut in which Smith read his Bible, Doctor Bruin walked slowly along the edge of the sand beside the glossy calm of the evening sea. To his right a few late bathers were splashing in the water before joining the night shift which was assembling to go out.

Yoshimitsu encouraged sea bathing. He said that it helped to keep down skin disease and spared the island's rather short supply of fresh water.

Doctor Bruin was not looking at the bathers. He was thinking, as he often did, of his wife and children.

After his marriage he had set out, objectively, to have a family of four.

He had realised before he had married her that his wife was a woman of easy-going, rather indiscriminate sexual appetites, and he loved her for them because they were typical of her friendly, generous character. He loved her, but without quite approving of her amoral attitude. That was why there had to be a family of four. He intended that through the children his wife should be kept busy and that her natural love of companionship should find an outlet in her home.

Before the capitulation of the Dutch Government in Java to the Japanese, he had been able to get her away with the children to Australia.

By now the youngest girl—they were all girls—would be five and the eldest thirteen. Without their mother the girls would be almost self-sufficient. The eldest would be able to look after the youngest and the youngest would be of an age where she could join in with the games her sisters played—a situation which would leave their mother a lot of spare time.

In Bruin's love for his wife there was a deep tap root of jealousy. He was too honest with himself not to recognise this sentiment and it troubled him a lot, for it was one that in a prison camp grew into an ugly, profuse weed the moment it was allowed to show its head above the ground.

As he walked he was trying, therefore, to avoid thinking of his wife as being free, trying to feel that she was beside him and that he could talk to her and perhaps lie with her when he reached the privacy of his room.

This daydream was interrupted when he saw an Indonesian coming towards him with whom he had had a lot of trouble.

The man was an advanced case of one of the forms of vitamin deficiency diseases. Being otherwise apparently healthy, he was horribly deformed about the mouth. His lips looked as if they had been turned inside out and inflated. Between them protruded, similarly inflated, his tongue. The surfaces of all three were crusted with dried whitish sores like closely seated barnacles on the smooth, curving red bottom of a ship.

Doctor Bruin knew all about the disease and how it could be cured. He needed citrous fruit or a citrous concentrate. He could obtain neither, so his patient would die.

The man was a native of one of the wilder parts of Sumatra. He was primitive, unschooled and had been brought up to believe that white man's medicine was comparable to the spells and charms of the old witch who lived alone on the edge of his kampong in the Sumatran hills. He was sure that had the Doctor desired it, he could have cured him almost on the instant. He was equally sure that the Doctor did not cure him because he did not want to.

His infirmity caused the man much pain. Also it made him mute and able only to produce gurgling sounds in his throat.

Quite respectfully he handed Bruin a piece of paper. On it were the words, "My friends in my hut say that they will kill you if you don't cure me. They say that if I were a white man you could do it, but because I'm black you won't."

Doctor Bruin acted on impulse. He crumpled the paper in his hand, threw it on the ground and walked straight past the Indonesian towards his hut.

Then he turned back. The man was looking after him with a wide unhappy stare.

Doctor Bruin felt ashamed. He realised immediately that the note meant nothing except that the poor wretch had probably lain awake suffering all night, wondering how he could persuade one of the doctors who administered the white man's medicine to save him from pain and the choking death that seemed imminent.

Doctor Bruin went back to the man and put his arm round his shoulders. With difficulty, because he found his throat was inclined to contract, he said:

"Jongen, jongen . . . I'm sorry. But as I've told you, I have no medicine for you. There is nothing I can do except to tell you again to bathe your mouth with warm water."

The man twisted in his arm, unbelieving, wanting to move away.

The Doctor held him firmly and added: "Listen, jongen, perhaps it might help you a little if I tell you this. The Commandant is a white man . . . and he is dying . . . and I cannot help him. He is my friend, my brother who shared my sleeping mat. I am helpless to help even that man."

The Indonesian turned towards him, grotesque mouth, cheeks wet with tears that he had been shedding for himself, wide, incredulous eyes. He shook his head.

The Doctor nodded. "Yes," he said, "it is true."

Then he gave the man's shoulder a slight squeeze and left him.

The hut which Doctor Bruin shared with the other doctors, the Commandant and the English priest had originally been the home of the Chinaman who had run the small rubber estate that existed on the island before the arrival of the Japanese.

The Chinaman had not been a rich man; his house was very modest. There were four small, ten-foot-by-seven rooms flanking a bigger central room that ran right through the full depth of the building. This central room was used as a store-room for any perishable or thievable stores belonging to the Japanese Command. In the space that was left, the doctors ran a small dispensary and, on rare occasions when they were necessary, carried out surgical operations or extracted teeth. One of the small rooms was set aside as an emergency ward where men who needed difficult surgical dressings or other specialised treatment could be kept and attended.

In front of the building was a narrow verandah where the doctors ate and foregathered when they were not working. Besides Bruin and DeGoyer there were six.

All the exterior walls and the partition walls of the house were built of heavy mahogany boards. The roof was of corrugated iron. Over the verandah grew a pair of big jasmine creepers. A few paces away from it were four great bushes of gardenias, all planted by the original owner.

From the verandah it was possible to sit and look out to the west across the tidal strait separating the island from a larger one in the group, some six miles off. In the evening the air was full of the sweet, heavy smell of jasmine and gardenia.

Doctor Bruin walked slowly into the room he shared with Smith and was disappointed to find him in. The spell that the Doctor had been weaving as he had walked by the sea was completely shattered. First the Indonesian had broken into the bubble that he was about to inhabit with his wife, and now there was Smith.

The latter looked up from his reading and produced a feeble smile. "Hullo," he said.

"Hullo," replied Doctor Bruin, and sat down. He had no

intention of holding a conversation and prepared himself to set about stifling any inclinations Smith may have had in that direction.

Smith looked at him curiously, sensed the antagonism in the Doctor's attitude, looked at the smoky mahogany wall in front of him, then back at the Doctor. Finally he leant back with his head against the wall behind him and closed his eyes.

In a way he was grateful that there was no need for him to speak, for he had nothing to say. At the same time, because of the Doctor's hostility he felt miserable. Smith was hungry for diversion and also full of a need for companionship. He remembered with melancholy the long, companionable silences he had shared with his mother in the mission-house drawing-room when he had been a young preacher in a colony in West Africa.

With a sudden jerky movement he picked up the piece of grey baft he used as a towel and went out to bathe. He hated the sea, but down on the beach at least there was noise and distraction.

Doctor Bruin frowned as he watched him go. Smith was not the smallest of the burdens that he was going to have to take over from the Commandant, who always spoke of the priest as "Young Smith" and patronised and cared for him because he thought him innocent and likely to take harm from the worldliness of the majority of the men in the camp. Doctor Bruin was not as generous as the Commandant in his opinion of the priest. He had amused the old man by saying idiomatically that he considered him "a bigoted young God-botherer".

Without thinking of what he did. Doctor Bruin picked up the book with the shiny black cover which the Commandant had given him earlier that day. Idly he ran its pages through under his thumb. It was full of the Commandant's rather eccentric handwriting, and as a book heavy for its size.

The Doctor could not make up his mind whether to start at the beginning and read straight through it or whether to pick a page here and there. As he lay back and raised it to a more comfortable position before his eyes, a loose leaf fell out of the front cover.

Doctor Bruin picked it up and looked at it. It was a letter written to a man called Bradford who lived at an address in one of the Southern Counties of England.

"Dear Brad," it said. "I hope that this letter reaches you and that one day, preferably on a winter's evening when there is sleet and rain outside your windows, you will sit with your stockinged feet steaming in the fender and read the book that accompanies it.

"Do not be distressed because they both come from one who was your friend and is dead. What I am sending you to read is a record of my thoughts and actions while I have been undergoing this experience of living at a level of existence that would have been inconceivable to either of us in the days when we pottered about the South Coast together in your nice little yawl.

"I did not write these notes with you in mind as their ultimate reader. Most of them were written when I still thought I should survive and that they would provide an interesting memento which I could read in later years and, perhaps, see then in a better perspective than I do now. But having written them and having realised that my days are numbered, I feel that of my few friends you would appreciate them most. Take them, use them in any way that you like and look on them as proof of my appreciation of the many pleasant days we spent together when we were younger and free.

"Your friend,

"Huth."

Doctor Bruin frowned and tucked the letter back in the cover. Then he turned to the first page.

In places leaves had been torn out of the book, it seemed indiscriminately. This had happened at the beginning, so that the notes started in the middle of a passage.

". . . with much confusion. From the bushes," Doctor Bruin read, "I could watch the activities of the Japanese ground and aircrews. Jimmy was just behind me. We were within twenty feet of the path used by the guards. Once an hour a squad of men passed so closely that I could smell the oil they used to clean their rifles.

"At night we were both afraid to sleep in case we made some sound that would attract their attention. The Japanese, as we had seen, killed escapees rather untidily.

"To reduce the chances of our meeting that kind of a death we had with us enough of a native poison to do away with ourselves . . . but only if we got the chance to take it, if we were awake. So sleep became another enemy to be avoided as carefully as the Japanese.

"Our plan for escape depended upon two things. First on being able to climb unnoticed into one of the aircraft we saw lined up every evening on the aerodrome, so that Jimmy could examine and learn the positions of the various cockpit controls. And then, on finding an aircraft deserted, fuelled and ready for flight.

"Used sparingly we had food with us for four days. A hundred yards behind us in some more bushes was a piece of bent corrugated iron which caught the daily rain . . ."

The Doctor skipped some paragraphs. He knew the story of the Commandant's attempted escape and how it had ended with Jimmy, the pilot, being killed by a guard and the Commandant's lucky opportunity to return to the camp undetected.

He went on reading again on the back of the next page.

"I had not been running away from the Japanese, or only incidentally. I had been trying to escape from living at too close quarters with my fellow men, English, Dutch, American, Chinese and Indonesian. I had not been trying to escape from any one man or 'man' collectively. That would have been impossible. I had been trying to escape back to a world where the veneer of manners and traditions, that makes existence in a tribe or community bearable, had not broken down.

"In the beginning, I went into prison camp with a good deal of hope.

"Between the capitulation in Java and my own capture I had time to consider what being a prisoner of war was going to mean. For two months I was, with a small party of other men, free.

"I came to the conclusion that captivity ought to bring the best out of men. Faced by the same common enemies, fear, indignity, boredom, hunger, discomfort, perhaps intolerance and distrust, they should be able to forget their differences and live together generously and honestly.

"Then our escape party was betrayed and we were taken into a prison camp. Believing what I did at that time, it was with excitement that I heard the grey steel gates of the compound close behind me. Also, it was with a feeling of relief, because those two months of being hunted had been a time of uneasy furtiveness, a time when we were suspicious of everything that moved and were the object of suspicion to every man who saw us. At last we were able to sink back into a crowd of people of our own race, all shaped together by being in the same predicament as ourselves. There we lost the feeling of loneliness, which none of us had recognised as loneliness while we were free.

"For a few days I still carried my excitement and my idealistic dreams with me. Then gradually they began to crumble. Before long I had pitched from hope to despair.

"The men who were with me had been prisoners just those two months longer. Yet they were already settled into the pattern that even now, as I write, is the one that dominates the entire structure of their prisoner-of-war lives. In a few words it is this: the fight for individual survival. Life in a Japanese prison camp converted men, who would have called themselves civilised, into animals that were prepared to prey on each other.

"It was when I had reached this conclusion that I tried to escape.

"I persuaded Jimmy that if we could get out of the camp and away to the airfield half a mile off we might manage to fly an aeroplane from Java to Australia. I convinced him too why it was we should take the terrific risks entailed, and try to get away. I told him that if we continued to live as we were living then, and we survived, we should end as cross-grained men who had lost faith in everything.

"It was easy to convince him. He only had to open his eyes each morning to see that what I said seemed true.

"Poor Jimmy. But I can write with equanimity of his death now, because I know that it was inevitable.

"At the time I felt terrible, though the Japanese killed him quickly and mercifully.

"When I got back to the camp his death and my own defeat left me in a state of absolute carelessness. Nothing mattered. I didn't feel hunger and for days I knew nothing of the life that went on about me.

"The first thing that started the blood running in my veins again was hate, hate for the whole of my own race. I was totally unable to credit any single one of them with any generosity of spirit or intention. Each and all were kept alive only by the pricking of their physical needs and I determined to turn fire loose among them.

"I came up from the bottom where I had lain for weeks, fighting mad and without any equilibrium at all.

"Most of the men in the camp were those whom I had known only in defeat. I could not believe that so many men—there were nine thousand of us—could be so cowed and abject. I thought that the best way to stir them was to adopt an extreme of their own attitude. They, I thought, were grubbing along their paths of self-seeking survival: I would show them how even that activity could be carried out with éclat. From an apathetic nonentity who was prepared to shamble downhill to a grave, I turned into a self-seeking wild beast prepared to kill wantonly just for the sake of bringing some sort of crisis into the lives of those who seemed inert and oblivious to . . ."

There was a page missing.

Doctor Bruin put the book down with a smile. He had not known the Commandant at this stage of his internment and he tried to reconcile the character of the man who had lain so close beside him for nearly two years with the picture of the man that came through from the diary. They were different people.

The Doctor was about to pick the book up again when he heard an agitated voice in the distance, outside the hut, calling his name:

". . . Mijnherr Doktor."

The tone of the voice sounded as if the man calling was in great distress.

Doctor Bruin closed his eyes and braced himself. In a moment, pain and cramps came to his stomach, twisting the muscles painfully.

Each time it happened the Doctor told himself, interestedly, that this was fear. But fear which had taken the wrong turning and was affecting the wrong set of nerves. He had tried to overcome it by explaining its causes to himself.

'You are not afraid of physical pain,' he had told himself, 'or at least not this afraid of it. A beating from a Jap is a beating, a limited period of facing a barbaric attack on your person, but with no more suffering attached to it than perhaps a broken eardrum or a bloody nose. No, it is my helplessness in the face of the unreasoning, explosive quality of Japanese and Korean temperament, something which by training and tradition is corked down hard and therefore all the more shattering when it blows up. Men,' he had added as an afterthought, 'who will cut the lips off a cat because it steals a piece of fish might be capable of any sort of calculated sadism.'

With deliberation the Doctor controlled the twitching nerves in his stomach and got up.

But he hadn't been able to talk himself out of his fear. The force that drove him forward was one that he was too shy to acknowledge, one that time and time again had driven him and the old Commandant out to meet trouble, though every instinct of self-preservation had clamoured to hold them back.

Doctor Bruin carefully set his green forage cap at an angle on the side of his head and walked out to meet whatever the crying of his name might portend.

CHAPTER IV

THE island lay silhouetted against the sunset like a dark caterpillar on a sheet of pink, crinkled glass. Sergeant Yoshimitsu saw it from the landing barge in which he rode with the eye of a father returning home after a long journey. The island was his. One way or another, perhaps happily, perhaps with trouble, it would welcome him. He would move back into its centre, make his will known and then everything would settle into its proper channels again and flow smoothly round him.

Yoshimitsu was tall for a Japanese. With his sharply moulded, oval face and high-bridged nose, his lithe body and air of alertness, he did not look like a man born into a working-class family. There was nothing squat or plodding about him, he stepped lightly and was fine-drawn and sensitive. Yet he was the son of a shipwright from Shimonoseki on the north-west entrance of the Inland Sea.

As a boy he had made many trips with the fishermen who had sailed the boats which his father had helped to build. Now, like a sailor, he stood on the afterdeck of the landing barge with his legs apart and his body easily balanced to take the motion the gentle head sea gave to the planks beneath his feet.

He was young, no more than thirty, and full of a vigorous pride of race and of his own unusual quality.

True, he was subordinate in the camp to Sergeant-Major Tadgibanu and to the officer in charge, Lieutenant Nashimura, but it was he, Yoshimitsu, who ran the camp.

Tadgibanu was a much older man, interested only in perfecting his brushwork—he was a fine calligrapher—and in curing the syphilis he had contracted from a native woman in the Celebes. Nor was Nashimura concerned with what occurred in the camp. He was a conscripted schoolmaster who looked upon his appointment to be in charge of prisoners of war as a perfect opportunity to study the history of the

Industrial Revolution in Europe, a subject in which he hoped to specialise after the war.

In contrast to Yoshimitsu, he was a humble man who found it every day increasingly harder to believe that Japan could win the war. Since at the same time his loyalty to his Emperor was unshakable, he was also an unhappy man. He knew enough of Europeans to surmise that if Japan were defeated, the descendant of the Sun Goddess Amaterasu would be defamed and, at best, lowered to the level of a constitutional monarchy: at worst, completely obliterated. To avoid having to think of these things, he immersed himself every day deeper in his books.

So Yoshimitsu was left with a free hand in the camp.

His work there required of him all his energies and he donated them happily because he enjoyed the exercise it gave to his vigorous mind.

It seemed to him that he was all the time being asked to make bricks without straw.

The camp perimeter had to be guarded and he only had Koreans, who were lazy and growing daily more insubordinate, to fulfil these duties.

He had also to provide most of the labour to build an airfield from sickly, antagonistic prisoners of war.

The Japanese Major in charge of the work on the mainland had no illusions about who ran the camp on the island. He drove Yoshimitsu mercilessly.

The Sergeant was not an inhuman man, but to carry out his orders he might in turn have driven the prisoners to death in great numbers if the Commandant had not been there to persuade him that to maintain his labour force he must keep them on their feet, and also that fear alone was not sufficient to get work out of starving, dispirited men.

Yoshimitsu saw the sense of his argument and balanced it as well as he could against the normal usuage of the East—which looks upon coolie labour as something to be used prodigally, because over-population has made replacements cheap and the value of life something to be balanced against the number of katis of rice that are needed to sustain it.

In Yoshimitsu's case replacements were not likely to be forthcoming: they had been used up or shipped away to other parts.

The Sergeant, therefore, listened to the Commandant and

badgered the officers at the Japanese Commissariat with requests for more food, and the medical supply stores for more drugs. In this, as in everything he did, he was energetic and persistent. On several occasions he had his face slapped for impudence by harassed men who were finding it more and more difficult, in the face of the Allied blockade, to meet the ever-increasing demands for food and drugs being made by the growing Japanese garrison, the civil population, the prisoners and, at the same time, to fulfil the need to stock-pile against an anticipated siege.

On the days when he got his face slapped, Yoshimitsu returned to the camp in a temper and sent at once for the Commandant.

For an hour or more he would rage at the old man deriding Europeans, damning the Americans for forcing Japan into the war by strangling her trade and vaunting the courage and skill of the Japanese fighting men over those of the Allies.

The Commandant, knowing the probable cause of the Sergeant's ill-humour, remained impassive until the tirade began to run down and Yoshimitsu had sufficiently recovered "face". Then he would introduce the beginnings of a new problem. Yoshimitsu would seize on it and berate the old man again, using the new subject as his talking point, until he discovered that the Commandant had come not only with the problem, but with a solution to it and one which might often, in the eyes of the Japanese Command, reflect to the Sergeant's credit.

In his calm moments Yoshimitsu had a lot of respect for the Commandant. This was because the old man had taken the trouble to learn how the Sergeant's mind worked and was therefore able to speak to him in a manner that almost prohibited misunderstandings. There was no false pride in the Commandant's attitude to the Sergeant, apparently no guile, enough respect, and avoidance of drama and a sense of humour: all of which were carefully calculated to keep the Sergeant sweet.

Yoshimitsu stepped down into the hold of the landing barge as it approached the shore. For a long time he had been hoping to catch the guards when they were being careless in their duties. They needed smartening up, but were usually too clever to be caught seriously enough in the wrong for the Sergeant to use his authority on them.

Yoshimitsu had noticed from the landing barge that there was no guard on duty outside the guard-house. The guard should have turned out in full strength to greet him. If they did not see him coming, he knew he would probably catch them all inside the hut, gambling.

It was as he had hoped. They did not see him until he stood in the doorway of the hut. The effect was as of an explosion.

The guard commander screamed an order in the tone of a man who has unexpectedly trodden backwards with bare feet into the hot embers of a fire. The rest of the guard rose from their haunches in a convulsion that was more mechanical than human and stood rigidly to attention.

With the minimum of words, spoken very softly, Yoshimitsu lined the Koreans up in front of the guard-house. His restraint at that moment was as substantial and searing to the touch as fire bars in a furnace.

Then, without another word, he swept at the line of men with the fury of a cat fighting for its life. As he struck at them with both fists he shouted a stream of imprecations.

To an interested Englishman, watching the scene from the camp cookhouse, the Sergeant looked and sounded like Punch when he has been exasperated beyond reason by the stupidities of Judy.

Yoshimitsu hammered the faces of all the men of the guard indiscriminately. He was a man berserk, allowing himself the pleasure of riding his rage on a loose rein. Only after ten minutes or more, when he was physically exhausted, did he stop. Even then he was not too out of breath to continue to damn the men who stood with bloodied faces, but still stiffly to attention, before him.

Afterwards, he had no feeling of shame for his outburst. It had been deliberate, something he used as a weapon to mete out punishment.

His rage petered out only when he had turned away and started walking up towards the camp, and he left a trail of little muttered phrases behind him that crackled like sparks from hot steel.

Instead of taking the main path which led circuitously to the camp he took a short cut which took him through the cookhouse.

Jansen, who along with the rest of the cookhouse staff had been pretending not to watch the castigation of the guard, saw him coming and tumbled the cooks, woodmen and the light-duty men, who worked in the cookhouse cleaning vegetables, into a hasty line.

As Yoshimitsu approached he screamed as the guard commander had done, "Kyotski". And a moment later, "Kieri". At the first command everyone came to attention, at the second they bowed from the waist and remained with their trunks hinged forward at forty-five degrees and their eyes on the ground.

To Yoshimitsu their attitude was no more than one of the respect due to himself as the representative of a conquering race.

Among those with their heads bowed there were other thoughts. The Englishman saw in it a subject which, in the way he would tell it, when he got home to the Mile End Road, would buy him many pints of beer and cause much laughter. Burns, an American in the party, wanted to spit: to him the scene was humiliating, almost beyond endurance. It was like a nightmare that had haunted his youth, in which, watched by the rest of his classmates, he knelt and laid his cheek to the ground between the fat bare feet of the old black scrub woman who kept the floors of the schoolhouse clean. In the dream his shame was followed by a ghastly suffocating struggle as the old woman spread her skirts and sat on his head.

There was a struggle here too, a struggle to restrain the impulse to turn on the others beside him and damn them for their subservience to a race which he thought of as subhuman. His anger was, obliquely, with himself as much as with the others. Had they shown the will to flout the Japanese, he would have joined them. He had not the courage to do it alone, but was reluctant to admit this and blamed the others for not giving the lead.

Ultimately he always recognised his own weakness and when his anger died out it left him morose and with an ache for the warm, thick scents of his home in Georgia.

Whenever he thought of his home it was the smell of the sun-blistered paint on the porch of the clapboard house; it was of the suffocating smell of the bleached dust from the unpaved road that ran before it; it was of the resinous smell of the yellow pines and just occasionally, almost too heavy for the breeze that carried it, it was of the sweet, oily scent of magnolias.

Here in the camp the smell was of decay. In all the camps the smell was of decay. Some of the men who had died beside him when he had been drafted to one of the outer islands near Amboina had smelt of decay before they were dead. The clothes they had left behind smelt of it too.

The fat Jansen was bowing and scraping to Yoshimitsu. They were talking together in Malay and Jansen was saying between bursts of that language, "Arimasen Gunso Dono— arimasen." "Thank you, Sergeant Your Honour. Thank you."

"Jesus Christ!"

"Steady, Burny," said the Englishman. "Take it easy."

The muttered words made the Sergeant turn his head sharply, but after a moment's pause he turned back and went on talking to the chief cook.

Jansen was in appearance a replica of the fat, benign chef that is common to all advertisements for culinary specialities. Only his eyes gave his pink, smiling face away. They were small, restless and calculating. Despite the meanness of his character, he was a fine cook and had been in charge of the kitchens of one of the biggest hotels in the East Indies.

When the Japanese had discovered this early in his captivity they put him to work for them, under the supervision of a Japanese cook in case he should want to poison them. But to poison the men he cooked for was a thought that never entered Jansen's mind. He had an enormous appetite and, as cook to a Japanese officers' mess, he had a better opportunity to satisfy it than when he lived in a prison camp. In the end it was his appetite which was his downfall, for he was caught smuggling food into his quarters at night to sustain him through the hours of darkness.

As a punishment he had been sent to the island.

Jansen would do anything for food. His stomach craved it endlessly. When he had been cooking at the hotel, he had had no fixed meal times, ate no set meals, but was never without a spoon in his mouth tasting the dishes that his staff were preparing. The result was that his stomach and digestion had become conditioned to expect a steady flow of food all day long. Hunger therefore assailed him far more quickly and had to be borne much longer than it did those used to eating only three times a day. Unless Jansen was getting food *all* the time, he was hungry *all* the time.

Throughout his waking hours, and he was a man who needed very little sleep, all his contriving and scheming was directed towards one object, the satisfaction of his appetite. His belly was his remorseless master and he served it faithfully. Nothing else mattered, nothing else took pride of place.

When the Commandant had told Ven Reebek that morning that Jansen was "informing" to the Japanese, he had been right. What he did not know was that the mischievous information the chief cook gave was of no value at all, because it was all invented. Jansen was a man forging a currency with which to buy himself food, for there was not enough official currency in circulation to meet his needs.

There were, as the Commandant knew, others in the camp informing, but few of them were in such a good position as Jansen to collect and particularly to deliver information, for he was frequently alone with the Sergeant checking supplies of rice and the few other items of food that were kept in the food store.

Today Yoshimitsu had what he considered to be big news for Jansen, so big that he wanted the chief cook to proclaim it to the rest of the men in the cookhouse while he stood by and watched their reactions.

Jansen was happy to oblige. He shouted the magic word, "Nouri", which released the men from their attitude of obeisance and began:

"Mijnherren . . . de Japanse Sergeant heeft mij verteld dat de Japanse Generaal heeft gegeven aan de Kamp Commandant . . ."

The speech went on in flowery phrasing and rolling guttural syllables for a long time. When it was done the Englishman muttered to his American neighbour:

" 'Ee says the Jap General 'as given the camp a couple of pigs for Christmas. Blimey, eh? That means roast pork for us, chum."

But Burns might not have heard him: he was scowling again at Jansen, who was bowing his thanks to Yoshimitsu.

The Sergeant was gratified and put momentarily in a good humour. He had won some applause, perhaps even gratitude, from the prisoners, several of whom even made bows privately to him denoting their thanks.

The pigs were not really a gift from a Japanese general; they came from Nashimura, Tadgibanu and the Sergeant himself; but he announced it in the manner he had for two reasons. One of them he explained to the men. He told them that the Japanese army was as good as it was because the generals were capable of showing an interest in everyone under their command, even those who ranked as low as prisoners of war. The second reason he kept to himself: it was the fear that if the camp command showed softness or kindness to the men, it might be reflected in a slackening of discipline.

After a further exchange of salutes, Yoshimitsu walked away from his quarters and Jansen dismissed the cookhouse staff.

They moved off in small groups. Some went to work on the issuing of the evening meal, others back to their billet.

Burns walked alone.

2

The hut inhabited by the cookhouse staff adjoined the lean-to shed which served as a kitchen. It was built of palm leaves laced over a light-wooden frame.

Burns, apart from a negro, was the only American in the camp. He lived an isolated life of his own, not because he had none of his countrymen to share his captivity, but as a matter of habit.

Even in the fo'c'sle of the tanker in which he had been serving as a deck-hand when she had been torpedoed, he had been inclined to shut himself away from the rest of his watch. He was moody, brooding and thoughtful, but seldom communicated any of his thoughts to anyone.

When properly nourished he had been short and sturdy, with close-set brown eyes under a cropped head of dark hair. Now he was gaunt and gnomish His eyes, without losing their expression of deliberate retention, glittered irritably behind their thick lashes.

Burns' war experiences and captivity had made him more withdrawn and bitter.

Within a few days of Pearl Harbour, his ship had been sunk by a Japanese submarine. In the Japanese destroyer by which he had been picked up he had been well treated, but he had not been in the mood to acknowledge this at the time. He considered the Japanese attack on Hawaii a treacherous one, and he linked the sinking of his own ship with it as another piece of treachery.

Also there had been the terror of the hours he had spent on a raft while he watched many of his comrades drown in a thick, treacly sea of oil. The tanker sank in a calm sea. Burns had had the extraordinary luck to be standing by a life raft when the torpedo struck. He had climbed straight on to it. As the ship had taken a sudden quick, vicious heel to one side, he and the raft had been shot erratically into the sea. He had not even been properly wetted, only splashed. Soon the oil had started to come up. It had boiled to the surface in great bubbles like disturbed gases from ooze at the bottom of a stagnant pond. In the bubbles, which spread quickly and soon joined into a thick film almost as impermeable as a thin sheet of rubber, there had been small black knobs that split to show white teeth and gullets and that had cried horribly for help.

Burns had been physically sick from the fumes of the oil, but he had been able to help one or two of the men up to the raft beside him. They had all swallowed too much oil, which poisoned them. The one who had survived the longest died within forty-eight hours.

So far as he knew, Burns was the only man left out of the entire ship's company.

In the Japanese destroyer he had been given a camp bed, dry clothes and food and had been allowed to sleep or to lie semi-comatose as long as he liked. There had been no guard set over him, but he was always sent back to his place under the after gun-shield whenever he strayed away from it further than to the latrine.

Only once had he suffered what seemed to him a deliberate indignity. It was after he had been on board for a few days.

He had been sent for from the destroyer's wardroom and taken up there under escort.

From the scene that he had observed on entering the cabin, it had been evident that the officers had been celebrating.

The officer who had sat on the destroyer commander's left had spoken a slow, precise English.

At first Burns had been greeted with silence, while all eyes were turned on him, not so much with hostility as with a friendly contempt.

After a long while the English-speaking officer had said, "In the name of my Captain . . . good evening."

Burns had replied, "Good evening."

The officer had frowned, "In the Imperial Japanese Navy it is customary for a lower-deck rating to address an officer as 'sir'. Do you not follow that rule in American ships?"

Burns had stared sullenly at the speaker and had not replied.

The officer's expression had become more angry. "Very well," he had said presently, "you will be taught a proper etiquette later, I expect. We are fighting men here and not concerned with teaching prisoners of war their manners. You are comfortable and well fed?"

Burns had again refused to reply.

The officer had turned to the Captain and they had spoken together for a few moments. Then he had turned back to Burns. "The Captain says he is prepared to overlook your bad behaviour and I am to tell you why you have been sent for.

"Tomorrow the people of your country who are celebrating their festival of Christmas will have their luncheons spoiled by having to swallow at the same time the news that the United States Island of Wake was stormed and taken this morning by the men of the Imperial Japanese Navy. Where the 'Stars and Stripes' once flew, the wind and the courage of Japanese Naval Arms has unfurled the banner of the 'Rising Sun'."

Again there had been silence.

"Have you anything to say?"

"Yes, I guess so," Burns had replied. "I guess I would like to sing a song, if you gentlemen don't mind."

And without waiting for an answer he had stiffened himself into an attitude approaching that of attention and had started, "Oh, say can you see by the dawn's early light . . ."

Burns knew the words, but being entirely tone deaf his rendering of the "Star Spangled Banner" had been quite without tune.

The expression of the officers who had been sitting on the leather cushions behind the long table had not changed as they had listened. They had heard him through without interruption. When he had finished, the interpreting officer had again exchanged a few words with his commander and had then turned back to Burns. "The Captain thanks you for providing him with that interesting song. Now you may go."

As he turned away, Burns had thrown over his shoulder, "Good day, gentlemen. . . . May your dinners choke you and may you drown in your wine." He had felt pleased with himself. "So long," he had added.

After he had gone the silence in the wardroom had been unbroken for a few moments and then there had been a loud outburst of laughter. Burns by that time had been out of earshot.

3

Burns walked back from the cookhouse with his head lowered. There was no doubt about his hate for the Japanese, nor did he feel much more kindly towards the Dutch or the British. The Dutch he believed were corrupt and cowardly and the British little better. Also, since he had been brought up to despise coloured men, or men with coloured blood in them, he had no time for any of the Indonesians. Which left him in his own estimation alone in the duty of upholding the high principles that the others about him apparently failed to find normal or necessary.

Martin, "Pincher" Martin, a British naval engine-room artificer was the only man in the cookhouse to whom Burns ever spoke voluntarily. Martin was a man who laughed a lot, even as a prisoner of war. He had a lean cockney vitality that was unquenchable, and Burns found it possible to admire him for it.

Martin had once slapped Burns on the back and said:

"You're all right, cock. You can't 'elp it if you've always got your teeth clenched. Gawd made you that way."

Burns walked slowly into the billet. It had been his turn to clean out and sweep up in there that evening. He picked up the bound bunch of bamboo slivers that served as a broom from the corner of the hut where he had dropped it when he had turned out to parade for the Sergeant.

As he swept he raised a thin cloud of dust from the earth floor.

"Hey, der boy, put some vater on de deck ven you go sveepink."

Burns knew the voice. A surge of anger instantly rose in him. He swept on, shutting his eyes, restraining himself.

"VerDomme!" It was the same voice. There was a flood of bad language in Dutch and a remark which included his name and brought laughter from five or six other men who were in the hut at the same time.

Burns rounded furiously on his heel so that he faced the speaker. He was a man who, with his brother, cut down and split the rubber trees in the camp for firewood for the kitchens. Both of them were of exceptionally fine physique. They were true blood brothers, sons of the same father and mother. One was black and the other white. The Kunst brothers.

It was the black one who had spoken. He sat on the edge of the bedding shelf with his feet on the floor. His brother lolled further up the shelf. They were both favourites of Jansen's and were well nourished and in good condition, kept thus by their work, the extra ration they were allowed for doing it and the still further extra they used to filch through Jansen, out of the camp grain store or from the Koreans.

Burns, a sickly figure by comparison with the black man, stepped across the few feet of packed mud which separated them and struck him across the side of the face with the broom. The sharp edges of the fine bamboo left several parallel lines of blood across the dark skin that welled and ran together.

Where before there had been a low murmur of conversation there was a shocked silence.

In it Burns said slowly:

"You black bastard. You dirty nigger."

Kunst got slowly to his feet.

A little wind whispered through a hole in the palm leaf thatch, twitching a few of the fronds.

Then Kunst leapt. He took Burns by the throat. There was almost a foot of difference in their heights as they stood straining together.

Burns, even in temper, was a cool fighter. He managed to move in close enough to the big man to bring his knee up sharply into his groin.

Black Kunst let go and dropped to his knees, then folded over them, straining and making a queer forced sound in his throat.

White Kunst stepped across him, in his hands he had a

half-made axe handle. He swung it to strike sideways at Burns, and someone caught the head of it.

Kunst swore and turned to find fat Jansen standing behind him.

Quietly, in Dutch, the chief cook told the half-caste to stop fighting.

Jansen had not been in charge of a kitchen staff of twenty or thirty men without learning how to make men obey him. He was strong too, in spite of his corpulence.

Kunst put the piece of wood down, stared with murder in his eyes for a moment at Burns, then turned and knelt beside his brother who still sat, sweating with pain, on the floor.

Jansen turned to Burns. "All right, Burney," he said. "Dot vill do. You take your foul temper and sit wiz it outside. After I vill take you and Kunst to t' Commandant."

Burns' anger was already spent. He felt sick. He walked out of the billet, up and over the centre of the island and came down to the shore on the other side. There he sat on the bole of a fallen palm tree. A cooling air came to him across the lurid reflection of the sunset on the sea.

He felt tired, and presently slid to the ground, put his arms on the tree, cushioned his head on them and went to sleep.

CHAPTER V

WHEN Doctor Bruin got outside his hut he found that he had alarmed himself unnecessarily. DeVissar was calling him to come to see the Sergeant.

As they walked together through the dusk, beneath the rubber trees, there was the sudden patter of heavy raindrops on the leaves above their heads. In a moment the rain was coming down with all the sullen weight of a tropical storm. As Bruin and DeVissar ran for shelter towards the Sergeant's quarters, the earth at their feet turned to ooze and sucked at the soles of their wooden sandals. With the downpour there was a sudden and temporary lowering of the temperature, which chilled the two men and brought them shivering up the steps to the threshold of the doorless opening that led into the small room that Yoshimitsu shared with the Sergeant-Major.

It was a room at the end of a hut occupied by the guards and by half a company of prisoners of war. Matting walls were all that separated guards from prisoners and prisoners from N.C.Os.

Tadgibanu and his subordinate lived, ate, slept and worked in a space that was fifteen feet square. A quarter of the floor within it was closed off, making a cubicle in which the two men had their bedding mats. The rest of the room was divided by a gangway that was flanked on each side by two low rostrums. Any man stepping up on to either rostrum left his shoes in the gangway. There was no furniture, save two cut-down packing cases which served as tables.

Doctor Bruin, followed by the interpreter, paused as soon as they were within the shelter of the roof, which had wide corrugated iron eaves, and saluted.

The room was lit by two hurricane lamps that left dark shadows hanging like veils in the corners under the roof. The green tunics of both men were stained darker in big spots where the rain had fallen on them, and the sweat had made deep half circles under their armpits that spread backwards and forwards like crutch heads imprinted on their sides.

In the light of one of the lamps Tadgibanu, with a small towel tied round his head, was making flowing strokes with a brush and black ink on a smooth piece of board. By the light of the other lamp Yoshimitsu was filling in a printed form, making, at the same time, calculations on an abacus. Both men knelt, sitting on their heels.

The rain roared on the roof with the sound of many empty metal drums being rolled down a long concrete ramp.

Doctor Bruin stood waiting for the Sergeant to make some gesture acknowledging that he had noticed their arrival. The clatter of their clogs on the wooden steps might well have been covered by the sound of the rain. The Doctor was about to speak when Yoshimitsu looked up and beckoned to him to come nearer. Bruin and DeVissar went and stood at attention in the gangway facing the Sergeant, who continued to click the beads of his abacus self-consciously.

After a time and without looking up, he called out a few words to DeVissar.

The interpreter turned to Bruin and said, "He is asking if you know what he is doing."

Bruin shook his head.

Yoshimitsu pushed a sheet of paper across the matting so that DeVissar could look at it.

"Corvée figures," shouted DeVissar after a moment. "They are returns for the numbers sent out over the month in the working-parties."

Doctor Bruin knew at once what would follow.

"What was the average?" he shouted back.

DeVissar glanced at the form again. "Just over seven hundred a day."

"And last month?"

"Nearly eight hundred."

Yoshimitsu looked up. He knew a few words of English but no Dutch.

"The Doctor knows why I called him?" he repeated.

"I think he does," answered the interpreter.

"Well? How does he explain it?" As the Sergeant started to shout his query, the rain stopped suddenly. He smirked at being caught shouting in the sudden silence and waited for an answer.

"You want to know why there were less men working this month than last?" asked the interpreter.

Yoshimitsu sucked noisily through his teeth and nodded.

Tadgibanu drew three quick strokes, broad at the head and with fine even tails that tapered imperceptibly into nothing, then looked up to see how the Doctor would answer. The Sergeant-Major had a round, lined face, a thick black moustache and an avuncular expression.

"Nineteen men died last month," said the Doctor, "nineteen men who need not have died if we had had enough food and drugs. There are many more sick with beriberi." He could see that Yoshimitsu was not in the mood to create a scene. The Sergeant's trouble with the guards earlier had drained him for the moment of heat, but he was trying to work himself up again.

"Never enough men at the work," he started to shout. "Never. Never. Never. They lie on their mats and pretend to be sick, all of them. If I take a stick and go through the barracks most of them lying there too ill to go out and work get up and run from me. If they were really ill they wouldn't do that, even when I beat them."

Yoshimitsu had only once gone through the barracks with a stick, though from his words it would have seemed to have been a regular occurrence. On the occasion that he did take a stick to the sick men he had only got halfway through his second barrack when he had met the Commandant standing in the middle of the gangway blocking it completely.

Yoshimitsu had never struck the Commandant, never touched him in anger. There was something about the serene way the old man always stood before him when Yoshimitsu was angry and hitting out at others that made him feel almost ashamed of himself.

Yoshimitsu had talked to Tadgibanu about this feeling one day. The Sergeant-Major had grinned and said something about the spirits of the Commandant's ancestors being strong and defending him. Yoshimitsu had shaken his head and wanted to pursue the question further, but was put off by the Sergeant-Major's bantering.

He had gone to hit the Commandant in the hut that time, and found he could not do it. He had put his stick down and crossed his hands on the head of it as if it were a two-handed sword and remained staring at the old man. The Commandant, who was standing with his feet apart and his hands on his hips, had come to attention and saluted gravely, asking:

"Did you send for me, Gunso Dono?"

And he had smiled as if at a joke which he was sharing with the Sergeant. Yoshimitsu had found it hard not to smile with him. He had kept a straight face, however, and ordered the Commandant out of his way.

The Commandant had obeyed him and then followed the Sergeant, right at his elbow, as he had walked down on the hut. At each man who lay on his bed sick and who now kept his bed when he saw that the Commandant was accompanying the Sergeant, the old man explained through the interpreter just what was the matter and why the man could not work. With beriberi patients he demonstrated their loss of reflexes; he took bandages off tropical ulcers; he compared the finger-nails and eyelids of those who were chronic malarias with those of the Sergeant himself—holding a mirror so that the Sergeant could turn back the lids of his eyes, look at them for himself and then compare them with those of men in whom an attack of fever every fortnight was destroying all the red blood cells.

Yoshimitsu was not a tyrant. Like most Japanese, he was overwhelmingly curious about things which were new to him. That day he learnt a lot of the elementary symptoms of the common camp diseases. His tour of the barracks, which had started out with the purpose of producing more men for the working-parties, ended with his promising to try to persuade the Japanese Command to provide more drugs.

Yoshimitsu came of a race that is trained to think of physical suffering as something to be ignored, in himself or in others. So he was not concerned with the sentimental side of the picture of sick and dying men, but with the common-sense argument that the Commandant kept putting before him that diseased and starving men were incapable of working properly.

"You," the Commandant repeated to Yoshimitsu almost daily, "want more men in the working-parties. Then get us more food and drugs and you shall have them."

At the same time the Commandant instructed the Dutch officers, who took the men out, to see to it that they did as little actual work as possible on the airfield. "We want to save the lives of the men in the camp," he said, "but not at the cost of those of our people who may be killed if the airfield is ever completed and used operationally."

"If we could get more quinine and B)," said Bruin for perhaps the hundredth time.

"B1—quinine, B1—quinine. Always. Always. It is like the song of the cricket, the same thing over and over again. I cannot get the drugs. You have to get the men well without them. There must be more men in the working-parties.

"You are the chief doctor in the camp. You are the one who is supposed to keep the men healthy, not me. If the doctors do not do their work properly and keep the men well I shall have to cut their rations. I must have nine hundred men tomorrow, you understand? It is an insult that over half the men in the camp are too sick to work. You must tell the Commandant I say so and that more men must go out to work tomorrow. Nine hundred—no less."

Yoshimitsu paused for breath and to allow the interpreter to catch up. Then he asked if it was understood.

The Doctor introduced a diversion:

"I shall not be able to tell the Commandant. He is too ill. He is dying."

DeVissar's look of astonishment as he translated was reflected in the faces of the two Japanese.

Tadgibanu rose and came over and stood behind Yoshimitsu. Both of them stared at the Doctor for several seconds without speaking.

Eventually Yoshimitsu asked:

"How soon will he die?"

The Doctor shook his head. "I do not know," he replied. "Soon, perhaps a week, perhaps less."

The two Japanese talked together, then Yoshimitsu went to a small haversack that was hanging on one wall. From it he took two sealed glass vials.

"Take these and cure the Commandant with them," he ordered.

The Doctor looked at the vials. Each contained $2\frac{1}{2}$ c.c. B1 concentrate. Enough to put, perhaps, two beriberi cases on the road to recovery.

The Doctor took off his glasses, polished them slowly and put them on again. He wondered how long the drugs had been hanging on a nail in the Sergeant's haversack. He said:

"Thank them, DeVissar. But tell them it might be too late to save him."

Yoshimitsu moved forward aggressively, angrily, his hands swinging by his sides.

"Cure him," he shouted. "You are a doctor."

Tadgibanu said something in a low voice. He knew more about injections and doctors than his subordinate. It was the camp doctors who injected salvarsan into him every few days, a drug the Sergeant-Major procured through a friend in the medical supply depot.

Tadgibanu's words to the Sergeant had a restraining effect. The Sergeant-Major waved at the Doctor and the interpreter, signalling that they should go.

As they saluted he said:

"Do not forget the nine hundred men."

Bruin and DeVissar had just reached the door when he called them back.

Yoshimitsu, looking out of countenance, stood back a little behind the Sergeant-Major.

"Anoné . . ." The older man's voice was pitched in a more gentle tone than Yoshimitsu's and he spoke slowly so that the interpreter should not have any difficulty in following him.

"There are two pigs coming into the camp with the working party in the morning. They are a present from the Japanese Command to the prisoners." He paused. "That is all," he added, dismissing them again.

Bruin and DeVissar were almost too surprised to speak. Bruin said:

"Tell the Sergeant-Major we are grateful."

Both Tadgibanu and Yoshimitsu ducked their heads in acknowledgment of the Doctor's and the interpreter's renewed salutes.

Outside as they walked back over the slippery laterite to the Doctor's quarters, DeVissar remarked, "Two of these little local pigs won't go far among two thousand men."

"Their fat will flavour the rice and we should get a shred or two of lean meat each and some soup," replied Bruin.

"What about the medicine, Doctor?"

"The Japs are idiots. Yoshimitsu has probably had this since the time he went out ten days ago, promising he would bring us back enough for all the beriberi cases in the camp. This was all I expect he was able to get. Having made such big promises, he was afraid that he would lose face if he came back with only enough for two men."

"And is it too late for the Commandant?"

Doctor Bruin turned and looked at the interpreter, frowning. "I don't know," he said. "I am rather afraid it is. We shall have to wait and see."

2

By the Commandant's bed-space there was a hurricane lamp. It was one of the two that lit the hospital barrack. The other barracks were allowed only one each.

Confronting each other in the light of the lamp were the Commandant and Jansen. The old man with his puffed and swollen face looked like a bad caricature of the chief cook.

The Commandant's breathing was so laboured that his intake of breath whistled a little in his teeth.

"Well, Jansen?" he said.

"Trouble, Kapitan," replied Jansen. "Big trouble. Dot Burns vas goink to keel de black Kunst. Zere vas som argumentink and he vas to keel 'im vis 'is 'ands. Also 'ee kallt 'eem a neeger and a blotty black bastard."

"This is bad. What did you do?"

"I stop zem fightink, Kapitan, and come to bring zem to you."

The Commandant looked down the hut and then back at Jansen.

"You do not like Burns, do you, Jansen?"

"Oh—ja, now—he works vell——"

"But?"

"He is difficult vit de men. He iss like I don' know vat— a scorpion perhaps vat strike eff you so toch heem vit a vedder."

The Commandant was silent, waiting for the sounds he had heard the Dutchman make to penetrate.

Nothing came through.

It did not matter anyway. There had been a row and he would have to settle it. He would listen carefully to what Burns had to say, for that would be the truth.

"Send the American to me."

"And black Kunst, Kapitan?"

"I will see Burns first."

"Ja, Kapitan." Jansen saluted and rolled heavily away down the aisle between the bedding shelves that held many men who had originally, weight for weight, been the same size as the chief cook. Now it would have taken any two of them to balance the scales against him.

Jansen found Burns still asleep with his head pillowed on his arms by the fallen palm tree. He woke him and told him to go to the Commandant.

Burns was shocked when he entered the hospital barrack and saw the old man. He had not seen him for weeks, had heard he was bad, but had not realised he would be anything like the sight he saw.

"Hullo, Burns," said the Commandant cheerfully.

"Er—hullo, Captain," replied Burns. "My, but you——" then stopped. He was going to say, "But you look sick."

The Commandant said, "Sit down by my feet there; we have to talk."

"Yes, sir," said Burns.

"Well?" queried the Commandant. "What happened?"

"Oh, Jesus, Captain, I got sore again, I guess. That nigger Kunst said something in Dutch that I didn't understand and he tied my name up with it and made some of the others laugh. I guessed he was being smart at my expense and that made me mad."

"So what did you do?"

"I hit him in the face with the broom I was using. It made a lot of little cuts on his cheek."

Somebody was rattling a spoon on a tin dixie to try to attract the attention of one of the orderlies. The Commandant waited until the noise stopped.

"And he went for you?"

"Yeah—got his hands round my throat. He is a big guy, Captain."

"So what did you do?"

"Brought my knee up in his balls."

"Go on."

"Then his brother came for me with a pick-axe handle, and Jansen stopped him just when he was about to take a crack at the side of my head."

The Commandant had made a tremendous effort and got every word of it. Now he found his head clearing; he was running into a lucid patch. The effort he had been making had done him good, at least temporarily.

69

"You are going to have to apologise to Kunst. You realise that?"

Burns was silent. He glowered out of the door frame beside him into the growing darkness. There was silence out there, no noise from the trees or insects. It was airless, the world had stopped breathing. Then there came a few great heavy drops of rain that fell like tears of mercury and were followed by the thundering deluge which was making speech difficult for Doctor Bruin and Sergeant Yoshimitsu across the way in another hut.

The Commandant, watching Burns, thought he looked like a spoilt child who is just about to be rude to his mother.

The old man beckoned, so that Burns leant nearer to him. Shouting, he said:

"If you do not apologise I shall have to take you out of the cookhouse and send you out to do coolie work with one of the ordinary working-parties."

Burns turned and looked the Commandant in the face, and shouted back:

"I never did understand, anyway, why you put me in the cookhouse."

The Commandant closed his eyes. There was a little spark of irritation within him that he wanted to keep under control. Burns was making time before he answered the order to apologise. The Commandant decided to give it to him. He relaxed. The rain drummed on the corrugated iron. Then it suddenly stopped.

"Well," he said, "I had two reasons. Number one, when I chose the cookhouse staff I did it so that all the races and nationalities of people in the camp were fairly represented. There are only two of you Americans here, one black and one white. That black boy, 'Snowball', is not very intelligent and at the same time is still in pretty good fettle; he can work outside all right. At fifty per cent, the Americans have a higher proportional representation in the 'keuker' than any other group in the camp.

"My second reason was so that you could join up with two or three others and provide a leavening of honesty there. The men in this camp are about nine out of ten corrupt. I had to have proportionate representation in honesty too."

Burns drew his brows together, screwing his eyes up. He bent and picked a small pebble off the beaten earth floor and threw it out through the doorway into the darkness. Then he said:

"Say, you're not really like a Britisher at all, are you, Captain?"

"Do you imagine that by saying that you are paying me a compliment?"

Burns frowned. "Why, I certainly meant it to be a compliment."

The Commandant laughed. "Oh dear," he said, "never mind. Tell me, how would you take it if I said you were not really like an American? Would you take that as a compliment?"

"I'm sure glad, anyway, that I am an American."

"Why do you dislike the British?"

"I guess they are so full of bull-shit, that is why." He paused. "Look, I was in another camp where there was a British officer in charge and he wouldn't listen unless I said 'sir' every few seconds."

The Commandant grunted. "And you think I'm not really like a Britisher because I don't make you say 'sir' to me?"

"Oh, and you don't tell me 'Stand to attention when you speak to me' and things like that. You just say, 'Come in, sit down', like they might back home."

The spark was getting bigger, the Commandant could feel it.

"I take it, however, that you do not like to call each other comrade—er—back home."

"We don't like to call anyone anything. If you call a guy 'sir' you are acting as if he was superior; if you say 'comrade' then you are right down there with him. Having to call people fancy names fixes your position. We don't have any fixed positions. Today I may be the guy that puts the driving mirror on the automobile in the production line, tomorrow I may be the guy that owns the buggy. And even when I ain't the boss, provided I've got dollars, I can buy the same things with them as he does, though maybe not quite so many of them."

The Commandant was tiring as well as getting angry. "So it all boils down to a question of dollars. Jones has a wireless set, you haven't. Tomorrow you may have enough money to buy one—then you will be equal to him. If you once call him 'sir' you can never be equal to him—so the situation must remain open just in case you find a way to make more dollars. Well, it's your way of life, thank God. And now, what about Kunst? Are you going to apologise?"

Burns looked at the Commandant for a long time. Finally he said, "Why, I guess if you say so, I have to, Captain."

"Send someone for him, will you? I want you to do it here in front of me." Again the sulky look came into the boy's eyes. "O.K.," he said, "O.K."

The Commandant did not feel that the interview was going very well. What did an apology in these circumstances mean? Practically nothing. There was a cold, hard lump of hatred in the American for a black skin that had formed in his cradle. In the half-caste there was a sense of slight that was raw and made him jump defensively into violent tempers. The cleavage went too deep for a mere apology to heal it—but what else could be done? Punishment? How could Burns be punished for something that he had learned from the example set him by his father and his father's father? And Kunst? Whatever slighting remark he had made about the American boy, it had been more than provoked by the months he had had to put up with Burns' unreasonable contempt.

Kunst came in, followed at a distance by the American.

The Commandant made another effort to speak with authority, but he knew it was a poor one even as he made it.

"Kunst, I will not have you fighting in the cookhouse, whatever the provocation. Do you understand?"

Kunst did not know the word "provocation". He did not really understand the Captain's English at all, but he usually caught the gist of what the old man wanted to say.

He stood stiffly at attention and said, "Ja, Kapitan."

"Burns is going to apologise, as he was the one who struck the first blow—but I am equally angry with both of you."

"Ja, Kapitan."

This is very feeble, thought the Commandant. I am not going to pull it off. What if Burns changes his mind now and refuses to apologise? I send him out on a working party, thus depriving the cookhouse of one of the few honest men in it and at the same time leaving this cancer open and festering.

Then Burns came forward of his own accord.

"I'm sorry, Kunst," he said. "I guess I have a mean temper. I hope I—er—didn't cut your face too bad or hurt you too much any other way."

Kunst was having a bad day with his English, but he saw from Burns' expression that he was making an apology.

"Iss all right," he said.

"Good," replied Burns and held out his hand. Kunst shook it without any great fervour.

The Commandant was grateful to Burns.

After the two men had shaken hands, they both turned and saluted the Commandant.

Burns' salute caught the old man by surprise. Then he saw the American was just playing a part, but playing it out of some kind of desire to please.

He let Kunst go, but kept Burns back.

"Yes, Captain?" asked Burns.

"Sit down again."

"Yes, sir."

The Commandant was silent for a long time. For so long that Burns looked at him with concern, wondering if he had had some kind of relapse.

At last he spoke.

"Burns, tomorrow is Christmas Eve. Tomorrow I am going to give up the command of the camp. I am too sick. I cannot put my mind to the job properly." He stopped and looked at Burns. "You are asking yourself what the hell this has to do with you. Only this, I am going to make Van Reebek my successor."

"Well, I'm sorry you feel you have to give up, Captain— but I guess being Commandant of the camp as well as being so sick is too much for anybody. And, why, I guess Van Reebek should do as good a job as anyone could in your place."

Burns was puzzled.

"I am glad you approve of my choice." For a moment there was a gleam of mischief in the Commandant's eye as he added, "Because, you see, he is a half-caste."

"What? You're kidding, Captain."

"No, I'm not. There is black blood in him. Almost any Dutchman will tell you that. But, make no mistake, he is none the worse for it, probably all the better."

There was another pause. Presently the Commandant asked, "Well, what are you going to do about it?"

"I guess you've got me snookered, Captain. What can I do about it?"

"Make up your mind," was the answer, "that you are going to be as straight and honest with him as you have been with me, and you may be very useful to him. And judge him by the goods he delivers rather than by the name he delivers them under. Will you do that?"

"I could try it, Captain."

"Good. Now you must go. I am tired."

Burns wanted to do something to express his sympathy and admiration for the man who lay before him, and could think of nothing but to stand up and salute again.

He felt foolish as he did it and he might have saved himself his pains, for the Commandant's eyes were already closed. Burns stood there for a moment wondering if he should speak again, then turned on his heel and walked out of the hut.

3

Doctor Bruin also had a hurricane lamp on the mat beside his bed-space. In his case, it was his turn to have it. The Doctor's hut was allowed one lamp for all its occupants. It was kept until nine o'clock every night outside on the verandah. After that each of the small rooms had it for one night, in turn.

The lamp stood on the bed boards between the Doctor and Smith.

The former was reading from the Commandant's book again. He read with a sense of pleasure. In the back of his mind was the knowledge that now, after all, the old man might live to re-read it himself.

"Most Europeans," the Commandant had written, "make no effort to understand the Japanese. They accept the 'East is East, West is West' dictum and leave it at that.

"I have made the effort. My contact with the Japanese has been close, but it has only been with a few of them and in a damnable environment. My knowledge of them is therefore very circumscribed.

"Much that I have perceived had had to be accepted with backgrounds that I have built in out of my imagination, so I have probably made many errors. Also I should not be human if I were not biased.

"I was lucky at the outset in meeting a Japanese who was highly educated and spoke good English.

"He was my interrogator after I was captured. He had been a professor of English and phonetics at the Waseda University. He had a better knowledge of English literature than most

74

Englishmen and a great personal respect and admiration for the well-known English poet under whom he had studied.

"Our introduction was abrupt, might have been unfriendly, was comic, and ended on terms of somewhat reserved friendship.

"My companions and I, after being arrested, were taken under escort from the police barracks, where we had spent the night, to a big building in the middle of the Javanese town of Sourabaja. It had been a college until the Japs took it over as one of several military headquarters.

"When we came in sight of the building our escort forced us, by prodding us with their bayonets, into a brisk jog-trot. We were taken, at the double, into a wide hallway and up two flights of stairs.

"The Japanese are not, to Western eyes, at their most elegant when they run. For their height, which is rarely more than five feet three, their heads are big, their trunks long and their legs ridiculously short. Most of the shortness of leg is in their thighs, an effect which is emphasised among their troops because they wind their puttees right up to their kneecaps.

"So it was at the stage where we were forced to double that somewhere inside me I started to laugh. It was rather shrivelled laughter, because I was very frightened. Press reports of the Sino-Japanese war had acquainted me with the kind of indignities and brutalities to which the Japanese were likely to submit European prisoners.

"At the top of the second flight of stairs, in a classroom, we were brought to a halt, having been doubled down a central gangway between rows of desks. There was a class in progress. The teacher with his forty or fifty pupils paid no attention to us. He behaved as if he were used to having a squad of men brought in at the double in the middle of a lesson. We were drawn up in a line facing a wall blackboard, with out backs to the class. The teacher, who was teaching the geography of Java to his Japanese pupils, was using another board on an easel.

"On the wall in front of us, written in beautiful, neat characters, was the pronouncement: 'As prisoners of the Imperial Japanese Army, you are now incorporated in that army in its lowest rank. It it therefore your duty to obey all orders given to you by all who wear the uniform of the Imperial Army.'

"For an hour while the class droned on behind us, we had to look at out blackboard without turning our heads away from it. If we showed an interest in anything else, the corporal in charge of our escort stepped smartly forward, screamed at the offender in Japanese and smacked his face, twice.

"The Japanese ably exploit the fear of noise that man has from birth. They use it particularly in their army routine to maintain discipline. The best N.C.O.s in their service are those whose voices have the greatest volume and power to strike terror. This corporal, the first Japanese N.C.O. we met, had learned his lessons well. When he reprimanded us his neck arched and his words came from his mouth with the sound of a mountain avalanche.

"A little while after the geography class had been dismissed I heard a new voice speaking Japanese behind me. It was one that belonged to an educated man. Our guards saluted and moved out of our line of vision. Then the voice said in English that was mechanically precise and correct in every intonation and stress, 'You may turn round, gentlemen. Step down from that dais and take seats at the desks.'

"We turned, and as we moved to obey these orders, a small, youngish man, without a jacket and wearing only a white cotton vest, crossed by the braces of his baggy uniform breeches, passed between us. He stepped up on to the dais we had just left. The lacings round the calves of his breeches were hanging loose and his feet, in white cotton socks, were thrust carelessly into a pair of cheap sandals. The general effect of his undress was that of a man caught unbuttoned in the privacy of his w.c.

"Lieutenant Inonitsu moved round behind a teacher's lectern and leant across it while he ran his eye over us. I noticed his hands. They were typical of nearly all his race. Fragile and delicate, they were tipped with nails that were the colour of cherry blossom petals and shaped like raindrops.

" 'I hope,' said the little man, 'that you have learned by heart the message that is written on the blackboard behind my head.' He looked at us over his glasses like a man burlesquing a country vicar. 'In case you haven't—let me see, you sir, must be Squadron Leader Williams—will you please read the words out aloud to us. Stand up.'

"Like a small boy, back again in school, I did as I was told.

" 'Good. Now that must be quite clear to all of you. To

test how quickly you are going to obey this order, I am going to have a question paper distributed. You will answer in full every question that appears on it.' He raised his voice. 'Tromp,' he called.

"A subservient and wretched-looking white man appeared with a sheaf of papers in his hand and started to pass them round. He carefully avoided looking at our faces as he moved among us. The man behind me stuck out his foot and tripped the fellow as he passed.

"Inonitsu was looking straight at the man as he did it. The Lieutenant raised his head and looked at the culprit through his glasses and it seemed to me that a smile flickered round the corners of his mouth. He said nothing.

"I glanced at my paper. The questions all concerned the military strengths of the squadron we had been serving.

"I was the senior officer present. I got up and said:

" 'I am sorry, neither I nor my men are allowed to answer this questionnaire. We may give you our name, number and rank, and nothing more.'

"Inonitsu looked at me in an impersonal way, then spoke at some length with the corporal, who was standing at the back of the room. Afterwards he turned to me.

" 'Squadron Leader Williams, you will accompany the corporal. You obviously have not learned your lesson, we shall have to take other steps to see that you learn it quickly.'

"I felt myself go white, but had no alternative but to obey.

"I was marched out and ordered to double. I had a man on each side of me and one behind. Like a corps de ballet in a bad pantomime we ran unevenly down the two flights of stairs and out through the echoing hallway. Though we passed through quite a gathering of Japanese officers, who stood in groups, none of them seemed to notice our passage. Then we ran over the footlights and down into the audience. In this case the auditorium was the street outside. There in the hot sunlight I lengthened my stride. I knew it angered my escort because they had to take two paces to my one, though I was not more than six inches taller than any of them. In this way, with the men beside me encumbered with rifles and bayonets and sprinting to keep up, I was taken the length of one side of a longish street and back up the other. The whole quarter had been taken over by the Japanese, there were no natives anywhere.

"I was brought to a halt in front of a guard-room. My corporal and the guard commander exchanged elaborate salutes and then I was ushered into a tiny cell behind the guard, who were seated on a row of chairs in a lobby.

"Five minutes later the two officers who had been with me in the escape party were brought in.

"One of them called out 'Hullo, Huth old man' when he was still standing in front of the guard. For this he was smacked in the face and kicked in the shins.

"In the cell afterwards we spoke in low voices. We were all very nervous and all tried to pretend we were not.

"We played a number of silly games to distract ourselves and told stories. Later we scratched a draughts board on the concrete floor with a trouser buckle, and with pieces of paper as draughtsmen we played innumerable games of what one among us who was a Canadian insisted was called chequers. Then we improved on that. One of us had the stump of a pencil and by writing on the pieces of paper we turned them into chess men. We spent thirty-six hours with only a bucket of water to drink from and a double handful of tiny biscuits to eat, before we were taken out of the cell again.

"We were then taken individually into the street and round the next corner to a small house where Inonitsu had his billet.

"The Japanese lieutenant's main argument this time was that we were mutinous, and he explained that it was the worst offence a man could commit in the Japanese or any other army, one punishable by death. We maintained that we had no allegiance to the Japanese Emperor but only to our own Sovereign. The argument that ensued was childish and ridiculous and we all got rather petulant, all except Inonitsu, who seemed to be enjoying a private joke.

"Twice more we were questioned, with intervals between questionings of twelve hungry hours. On the whole, the guard was indifferent to us. But there was one brute who amused himself by making lunges at us through the grille door of the cell with his fixed bayonet. As the cell was very little wider than the length of a rifle and bayonet, his actions caused us some anxiety and he once grazed the arm of one of my companions.

"My reception, on the third and last time that I visited Inonitsu, was totally different from the others. Instead of having to stand to attention and face him across a desk, I was taken into a room where there were easy chairs. He was seated in one and waved me to another. Then he called for Tromp and ordered him to bring tea and cakes. I was surprised, because the other two who had been in before me had not reported any change in the style of their reception.

"With me, Inonitsu was charmingly amiable. We never once talked about anything to do with the war. We talked of Shakespeare, of various English poets and of Laurence Binyon. He fetched books containing copies of the poems we talked about and told me of conversations he had had with several well-known figures in the world of letters. He was not showing off, merely discussing a common interest.

"Just before he dismissed me, I asked him two questions: the first, why our interview had taken the course it had, the second, why he had allowed my companions to be beaten by the N.C.O.s in the class-room and in front of the guard?

"To the first he replied, 'I talk to you as I do because it pleases me to talk with somebody who is interested in the same things which interest me. As you can imagine, there are few with such interest in the Japanese Army.'

"To the second, he said: 'It is the normal form of punishment in our forces; you will have to get used to it. We do not put people in cells or in solitary confinement unless there is no other way to discipline them. If we shut a Japanese soldier away from the sunlight and open sky we are shutting him away from something spiritual and the disgrace is so terrible that he will probably hang himself. We believe that punishment should be swift, memorable and unceremonious. Your Western way of depriving a man of his normal way of life for weeks, months or years is unthinkable. Beat the man, and at once, even if he is seriously hurt, he will be all right again in a few days and the punishment is done and over.'

"As I was going he did not offer to shake hands; I think he realised it would have been a false gesture. Instead, he handed me a small parcel. As he did so he said:

"'I have franked what it contains so that you will be able to keep it until you are released. Do not open it now. It is not the custom among my people to open a gift in front of the donor in case it is something unworthy or insignificant, though perhaps the best he could do. We give thanks for a gift, not for its material value, but for the spirit that moved the man to give it.'

"I was rather embarrassed by his lecture but managed to thank him fairly gracefully, and had just reached the door when he called me back again.

" 'Take some of these cakes,' he said. 'Where you are going you are likely to be hungry. Your European standards of eating are too rich for us. Our soldiers,' he added with a challenging look 'can fight all day on a handful of rice.'

"The parcel contained a copy of the complete works of Shakespeare in English.

"Later that day we were transferred to a prison camp on the outskirts of the town."

The Doctor put the book down and composed himself for sleep. What he had read had not impressed him particularly. There had been too much wanton violence and slaughter committed by the Japanese for him to feel that there was anything but exceptional luck in the contact that the Commandant had made at the beginning of his period of internment.

He closed his eyes.

After a moment he opened them again.

"If you get some B1 you will have to give it to youngsters like Wim Peterson . . . not to old dodderers like me."

It had not seriously occurred to the Doctor that he might not give the vitamin concentrate to the Commandant. But might not the old man be right? He had lived a large part of his life span. Mere boys like Peterson had gone behind barbed wire when they were no more that thirteen or fourteen. Who had the better right to an opportunity to live? Especially when the Commandant was so worn out that the dose of B1 might not save him anyway.

Part of the Doctor's strength was that he could shelve an anxiety until he was in the right mood and condition to deal with it.

Having registered his problem as something that had to be dealt with urgently the next day, he shut his eyes again and went to sleep.

4

Smith was also reading by the light of the same lamp that served Doctor Bruin. When the Doctor put down his book and closed his eyes the priest did the same.

He had been reading the Old Testament prophets and he felt exhalted by the same moral indignation that the old Jews had felt for the sins and pridefulness of their people.

Smith dreamed ahead to the conquests that he would make one day in the name of God.

He saw himself a plain figure, dressed as other men, yet clothed with spiritual light, moving among his converts.

"God bless you, my child: and you, my child: and you . . ." Simply, soberly.

The Bruin turned over and blew out the lamp.

The darkness cut across the radiance of Smith's thoughts and struck him between the eyes.

He was back in a Japanese prison camp surrounded by uncertainties. Would he have enough to eat? Would he die? Would God save him, as he prayed every night? Was God watching over him? Did he believe that God was watching over him? *Did he believe in God?*

Smith turned restlessly on his mat. He thought of his childhood in the strict nonconformist home where it had been a sin to whistle on Sundays. He thought of a passage he had made in a mail boat on the way to West Africa, when he had found himself lusting for a young woman who ate at the same table in the saloon as he did. He thought of the dry red laterite compound of the Mission house in the Ashanti with the harmattan overhead and the sky glowing like the inside of an oven.

He thought of anything that would save him from *the* thought. Did he believe in God? Think as he would, he could not escape from it. It was there all the time.

He was like a man shut alone in a dark room with a poisonous snake; he was frozen in terror, frozen, but knowing that sooner or later he would have to move and then the thing would strike.

CHAPTER VI

AFTER lights out in the rest of the camp the two hurricane lamps in the hospital were allowed to remain lit, but were turned low so as not to disturb those sleepers nearest them.

In one end of the hut, at this time, there was quiet. The beriberi and malaria patients slept fitfully, but without much pain. At the other end of the hut among the dysenteries the night was as restless as the day and there was a steady undertone of remonstrance and despair. Despite its many windows, the hut was airless and stale with the smell of death and near death.

Wim Peterson lay and stared at the beams above his head. In the dim light there seemed to be no roof above them and they might have stretched away into the darkness of the night sky.

More than three years earlier, when he was thirteen, he had lain staring up like this one night in the compound of his home in Batavia. He had watched the moon sailing through the sky, had seen the skirt on one side of a cloud glowing in its wake as it disappeared and then the skirt on the other side brighten and shine as it glided out again. He had wondered then, if he had been able to get up there and ride on the moon, what it would have been like and where it would have landed him. He wondered if, looking down into the dark night sea below him, he would have been able to see from the moon the long, pointed ellipse of his father's submarine sliding silkily after the Japanese transports that were bringing men and the materials of war to the Dutch East Indies.

Certainly, if he had trusted to the moon it would never have landed him here, never stacked him, a bloated beriberi patient, together among others with the same sickness, packed and skin-tight like a pound of sausages.

He wondered too where his mother was. When he thought of her, he saw her always in the same tragic pose that had been his last glimpse of her.

At first, after the Japanese invasion of Java, he had been allowed to go free with the other lads of his own age. Then he had been impounded with his mother when the Japanese had rounded up the women and put them behind barbed wire.

Finally, when he was just over fourteen and the Japanese were looking for more males to fill out their labour corps of prisoners of war, he had been drafted from that camp to one for men, and from there again, after only a couple of weeks, to one for military prisoners of war.

The last camp he had been in before being sent to the island was not a hundred yards from his old house in Welterwreden, near the Batavia airport.

On the day he left the women's camp his mother had stood with her face pressed against the squares of barbed wire on the perimeter fence and watched him march away with a dozen other youths of the same age and an escort of guards.

The tears had run down her face, met at the chin and dripped off it in a steady stream. Her voice, broken and choking, had called after him, "Good-bye, Wim. Good-bye. Come back to your mother one day. May God send you back."

When he had left her, his mother had not known whether his father was alive or dead, and at their parting she had lost her son. She had been so brave all the time until then, never showing her anxiety about the lack of news of his father's ship, or about the Japanese occupation—just living quietly and efficiently, thankful, perhaps, to be able to have her son with her.

Wim felt sick and so helpless. He was defeated, beaten, bound and condemned to die. He could not help himself and there was no one to help him.

He turned heavily on his side.

He thought about his father, and wondered whether he was still alive. He had been a jovial, laughing man, clever with his fingers. A cleverness he had passed on to his son, who, before his fingers had grown too thick and clumsy with beriberi, had carved little ships out of splinters of wood. Little ships that were so correct in detail that some of the older men, old seamen and sea captains, had commissioned him to make models of their ships for them, each one no more than six inches long. They had paid for the ships in kind with whatever they could afford, a pinch or two of tobacco, a handkerchief, two or three teaspoonfuls of sugar, an old tin that he could make into a cup and barter for something else he required.

83

Wim had been a typical little Dutchman when he had joined the men's camp. He was thin by nature, with hair that would have been silver if it had not shown yellow through the parting, and pale blue eyes.

He had inherited from his mother an instinct for dressing neatly and for keeping himself clean. They had made a fuss of him—the men—because he had seemed so new and delicate, was so good to look at, so slender.

Now he was likely to be among the next twenty or thirty to die, and was puffy and pasty like a suet pudding.

Wim closed his eyes and tried to sleep, but turned over on his back again almost immediately with his eyes open.

Sleep would not come just because it was bidden. Had it been possible to will sleep, all the men would have drawn it over themselves like a blanket as an escape from the realities around them.

A few, like his friend Bruckner, did not welcome sleep. They were the active, scheming ones in whom the powers of survival were strongest. They were energetic, mentally and physically engrossed in material things. Wim admired Bruckner and stuck to him loyally, though there were people in the camp who were afraid of the malignant intensity of the dark youth and hated him.

Bruckner was a year older than Wim and was not a pure European.

He was short and still sturdy. He had russet-red hair and thick eyebrows that almost met over dark brown eyes that were always calculating, always prepared to be evasive in the face of a direct glance, yet always on the look-out for the opportunity and the position from which to counter-attack. He was a little animal, without scruple and fiercely fighting for life. Knowing how he was prepared to act himself in this battle, he trusted no one.

Wim's loyalty and friendship Bruckner regarded as a material acquisition. Wim was popular, and his ability to make things with his hands was an asset. It earned goods that Bruckner could turn to their mutual advantage and it made it possible for them to have the tools to carry out all kinds of tricks that would end in providing food for one or both of them. The object always of all Bruckner's scheming was to obtain food. Clothing and other requirements such as soap or entertainment came a long way after the satisfaction of his

84

stomach's needs. Here again Wim made a good partner, because while he was pleased to have food, he could often be put off with something else, a nicely grained piece of wood, a book, an odd piece of lead, anything that would provide occupation for his mind or his hands, thus leaving the food for Bruckner.

Where the dark boy led, Wim followed.

There were coconuts to be had if anyone was prepared to break camp orders and climb for them. The Commandant had put a ban on the indiscriminate picking of coconuts because the medical staff had need of the milk. From it they made a yeast culture that was good for the beriberi patients.

Bruckner argued with Wim, who was just beginning to show the first symptoms of beriberi at the time, that he should have the milk and the flesh of the nuts to help him ward off a more severe attack.

So, secretly, on several nights, with one watching for the camp guards or anyone who might report them to the Commandant, the other scaled the palms and brought away coconuts.

Once Wim had been up a tree when a Korean sentry had come to smoke a cigarette in a nearby thicket and he had had to cling to the bare bole of the tree, unmoving, for twenty minutes until the man had gone. He had learned young, in Java, how to climb coconut trees and had been the official coconut picker in the women's camp, where there had also been a grove of palms.

Having got the coconuts, their difficulties were only just begun. They had still to husk the nuts soundlessly and then bury the husks. It was the first part of the operation that was the most difficult. Or it was until Wim, with a small triangular file, made something like a hack-saw blade from a piece of steel. Used slowly and carefully it made no sound and bit easily through the outer shell and into the soft fibres underneath it.

In the end they had been caught and brought before the Commandant, who had treated the whole matter in a very forthright way. He had not lectured them or asked for excuses, but had given them the choice of two punishments. Either three months continuously with the latrine-cleaning squad, a job which normally came round about once every month to each fit member of the camp, or a beating, to be administered in the presence of three officers, by Lieutenant Van Reebek. They had both instantly chosen the latter course, and were that evening bent over an old box and given half a dozen strokes with a bamboo cane by the muscular young Dutchman.

Wim had found it a painful experience, but the seventeen-year-old Bruckner had scoffed at it and muttered contemptuously something about the Commandant's attitude having been typically that of a "VerDomde Brit".

Bruckner was thankful enough, however, to the Commandant on the day the Japanese caught him and Wim outside the barbed wire boundaries of the camp.

Bruckner had organised the expedition to get the roots of a wild lily that were edible. The lilies grew in a glade about a quarter of a mile from the camp.

They had never been outside the wire before; and although they used every caution, they were caught as they came back by three Koreans who were off duty taking a stroll.

Bruckner had been badly frightened and had shown that once his initial bravado had been beaten down he was a coward. Wim unfortunately had not the perception to see this, but the Commandant had.

The two boys had been taken by the Koreans straight to Yoshimitsu.

DeVissar had come to the Commandant full of anxiety. The two boys would be executed for sure, he said, for such was the Japanese order that applied to those who tried to escape. Even the old man had been disquieted when he was told that they had been caught outside the wire.

When, however, he learned why they were outside, that it was not the madness of an attempted escape, then he drew a breath of relief and went to work to convince Yoshimitsu that it was no more than the prank of a couple of youngsters driven by hunger, seeking to fill their bellies. Yoshimitsu, who had been working himself up to beat the boys, saw that the Commandant was right.

After another half-hour of raising terror in them, he let them go without even slapping their faces.

When they had left his quarters, the Sergeant turned to the Commandant and asked him if he thought he had frightened them sufficiently to deter them from trying such an escapade again.

Rather grimly the Commandant said he thought he had,

but that just in case he had not, he, the Commandant, was going to discipline them himself.

To his surprise, Yoshimitsu had forbidden him to take any further action and had then pleaded the boys' case on the very same grounds that the Commandant himself had pleaded it earlier.

The Commandant had not argued with Yoshimitsu, but that evening he sent for the boys individually. He did not want to lose the opportunity of driving a wedge between them, for he knew that Bruckner was by instinct a delinquent and was afraid that a boy in Wim's position, rootless, growing cynical and with only a rather tattered remnant of conscience left, might be too easily persuaded into evil habits himself.

The Commandant faced a sullen Bruckner and told him that he considered him an enemy to the community, that if he misbehaved any more, or showed any other signs of flouting authority, then he would not hesitate to hand him over to the Japanese for punishment.

For the first time in Bruckner's life he was shocked. He was also alarmed. The Commandant, seeing his reaction, explained through Doctor Bruin, who was interpreting, that the un-written law which he had always observed—never to call in the Japanese to enforce camp discipline—applied only to those people who themselves did not break another unwritten law and provoke his authority beyond reason.

"I know," the Commandant had said, "that there are people in this camp who talk loudly about the right way to handle social misfits. I have heard Steensma give his lecture on how criminals can be rehabilitated by reasoning and kindness. I watched you at that lecture and I could see you hugging your-self with glee, because it left the whole world open for you to go in and plunder and thieve in any way that pleased you.

"I do not believe in Steensma's theories. I am here and you may come and talk to me about anything you like, anything that seems to you to be a difficulty or an unfairness—but—if you continue to lead the life of a thug and pirate, I shall not hesitate to take you by the ear to Yoshimitsu and have him flog the life out of you."

After Bruckner had gone Bruin said: "You did not really mean that, did you?"

And he was surprised at the hard glint there was in the old man's eyes when he said: "I should be guilty of gross sentimentality if I didn't. Please God I may never have to fulfil the threat. I shall go a long way before I do, but if in the end I can see no alternative, I shall be right in taking him to the Japanese. Now let's have a word with the Peterson boy."

With Wim Peterson he had been just as stern. He used the same threat to him as he had to Bruckner, only he left out all that he had said about the first boy being an enemy to the community.

Instead, he had shown how frightened Bruckner had been in front of Yoshimitsu and how unreliable a comrade was a man who was a coward and a self-seeker. And he had ended again quite firmly with his threat about the Japanese.

This time Bruin was really staggered. "You do not believe that it was necessary to snarl like that at Peterson?" he asked.

The Commandant looked his friend in the eye and said: "No. Do you?"

"But then, why?"

"Jan, what has come over you? Peterson will not go right out and make a break with Bruckner now. What I said about cowardice and self-seeking is going to take time to sink in, if it ever does. In the meantime Peterson will tell Bruckner all that I have said to him. When Bruckner hears my heresy, about calling in the Japs, repeated, he may think I mean it. He is clever enough to think that with him it was only a threat."

"But may not your tackling the thing this way undermine your authority? After all, your authority in the long run depends on your popularity."

"In the short run my authority depends on popularity," corrected the Commandant. "In the long run it depends upon the amount of power I can actually wield."

3

Wim Peterson had been outside the wire again, afterwards. It had been with one of the Korean guards, who had invited him one evening to accompany him. The Korean spoke fairly fluent Malay, a language that to Wim was as familiar as his mother tongue. The Korean was an amiable creature, known in the camp as the "Smiler".

Wim had told the man that he thought it would be dangerous. But the Korean had persuaded him, saying:

"If you are with me nobody will say anything."

Wim was reluctant to offend the man because it was possible through him to make purchases in the market on the mainland. The Smiler would also take things out and sell them. He had once taken some carved Chinese junks that Wim had made and had brought him back a very fair price for them.

So, though every instinct warned him that what he was doing was foolish, Wim went with the Korean and sat with him in a little bush-screened cove on the edge of the sand.

For a long time it had not been apparent what the Smiler's motive had been in bringing the boy out. The Korean talked a great deal about his home town in Korea and about his wife and family. All that he said was very sentimental and rather pathetic.

A great full moon rose over the mainland and let down a golden ladder which shimmered across the water to their feet.

At last, shyly and ashamedly, the Korean told the boy why he had asked him to be alone with him. He wanted Wim's body.

The decision which faced the boy was the most frightening one that he had ever had to make. Characteristically, though he was docile and easily led in almost everything, when he came to a point that really set him in a corner he could act with courage. He refused the Korean what he asked, and was surprised, relieved and almost happy to find that the man was not offended or violent.

As they parted, going back into the camp, the Korean had even put a moist, warm hand on the boy's arm and said:

"But we are still friends?"

And Wim, glad to escape so easily, nodded quite enthusiastically.

All these things, the inverted Korean, Bruckner, the tearing apart of flesh that had been his parting from his mother, the sickness, hunger and squalor that was all about him, had gone a long way towards reducing Wim to the state that he was now in. A mental state as well as a physical one, from which there was likely to be a long hard climb back if he were ever to regain normality.

Beyond all things that had affected him was, however, his trip with Van Reebek to the Hi-Ho camp.

Hi-Ho's were coloured men of Java and the other East Indies who enrolled under the Japanese army banner for the "Fight for Greater East Asia". The fine words that had caught them and brought them in had been simply a subterfuge of the Japanese to obtain labour. For a few weeks the men were drilled and occasionally given simple duties like guarding prisoners of war or marching through the streets of large towns to attract more recruits to the service. Then they were drafted away from their home islands to places abroad where they became, what it had always been intended that they should become, slave labour.

At times when Van Reebek was not on duty with the night shifts, the Commandant used to send him out in charge of what was known as the "Wandel Plug". This was a small, select party of men, all as healthy and strong as possible, who were used by the Japanese for odd jobs that lay some distance away from the airfield. They might be sent in lorries to a big town twenty miles away to fetch cement, or to one of the fishing kampongs up the coast to collect dried fish. On another occasion a boiler and boiler-house were being dismantled at a mine in the hinterland and the "Wandel Plug" had been sent to provide the labour.

It was a working-party for which there was seldom a shortage of volunteers. The men liked the voyaging that the work entailed, and in small parties, perhaps in the charge of Japanese instead of Koreans and often of men who were craftsmen, such as the boiler fitter who had taken them to the mine, there was less restraint and a more human approach to the work.

The engineer who had been in charge at the mines had bought out of his own pocket great cones of "gula malacca", local brown sugar. On another occasion two cartons of cigarettes had been divided up among the men. And on one day, after cleaning up the compounds round some Japanese military billets, the group had been allowed to listen to a gramophone for an hour and had been given a meal afterwards.

Most of those who went with the party were young, healthy Indonesians; few of the Europeans were ever strong enough to stand the long hours or the hard work they might be asked to do.

Wim Peterson had got himself on to several of the "Wandel Plug" parties. The last one had been when he was already showing the first signs of beriberi.

An unusual feature of this party had been that Doctor Bruin

and the sick bay orderly, Schiller, had been included in it at the request of the Japanese. They were taken a long way in a lorry and unloaded at the gates of what appeared to be another prison camp.

When they descended they had been struck at once by the foul smell that hung over the place and by the fact that the sentries, who stood in fairly large numbers round the perimeter, wore white masks such as nurses and doctors wear in an operating theatre.

Each of the working-party was at once issued with a similar mask and drafted straight in to work through the barbed-wire gates.

The camp had been for a labour force of Hi-Ho's who had been building another airfield. Cholera had broken out in the camp. There were over two thousand men in it.

When the "Wandel Plug" got there, about eighteen hundred were dead and unburied and the remainder dying.

The Japanese had done nothing about the condition of the men. There were no medical facilities; the nearest Japanese doctor was forty or fifty miles away. No one had recognised the disease for what it was until over a hundred had died of it.

Someone at Command Headquarters had then been informed and a corporal in the Japanese medical corps had been sent to deal with the situation. He had taken one look at the camp and had reported back that there was nothing to be done except to seal it off and thus prevent a further spread of the desease.

There was not anywhere sufficient drugs to begin to cope with the illness in the camp. The corporal had found over five hundred confirmed cases on his visit; at least another five hundred must have been infected and probably many more. To sort the sick and sickening from the healthy was quite beyond the limited resources of the Command, so it was simplest to write the whole lot off, build a new camp and enroll another two thousand men.

The "Wandel Plug" had been brought in to bury the dead and to burn down and destroy the camp and all that was in it.

Even the adults in the party were badly shaken when the situation was revealed to them. For Wim Peterson it seemed as if his mind was going to be unhinged by it.

To him it was like the destruction of the flying ants at home, when they used to come after rain and kill themselves in heaps in the flames of a small fire specially made for the purpose of attracting them—only now the bodies were human ones.

For those who were not already dead there was no one to fetch and carry. Crying usually for something to drink, they lay and died in their own excreta. Or crawling to the polluted stream that ran through the camp, they drank more poison and died with their heads fallen into the water.

With Wim's horror was the fear that he too might contract cholera and die as he saw the little Javanese men dying.

"Tuan ayah—Tuan—Tuan." The voices of those who were left called always for water.

The Japanese corporal, who was in charge of the operation, directed that the only water to be given to them was from the polluted stream.

The Japanese provided gloves for all who worked in the camp; gloves, masks and a new set of clothes every time they left the compound. Each man walked at the end of the day naked across open ground to a bath of disinfectant, leaving his soiled clothing in a heap for the last man to soak with petrol and burn.

The men of the "Wandel Plug" lived for the three days in a hut outside the camp and were given extra rations. After the first day they ate them hungrily and actually put on weight.

Wim worked in the camp with Schiller and Doctor Bruin, attending the dying, while the rest built huge funeral pyres of rubber-wood logs and stacked them with the rotting bodies of the dead.

The essence of Wim Peterson's impression was the realisation of the casualness of it all. The dead men might have been so many bundles of dried grass for all the concern that was shown.

Some of the men of the "Wandel Plug" were, within twenty-four hours, treating the whole thing as the Japanese had. They even joked quietly and sometimes laughed as they worked.

Wim, who had so recently left his mother's side, still remembered the care and trouble she had taken with him—and had seen the patient abnegation of other women with their children in the camp. He saw too the love that was poured out, the way women would give up their food so that their children, particularly their men children, should not go without. It was self-sacrifice that was not anywhere paralleled in the men's camps. It occurred to him that other mothers had given up part of themselves for these suffering coloured men in the same way—and for nothing.

Wim had, as he showed in his carving of little ships and in other ways, a strong feeling for design, for the functional purpose behind the creation of objects. What he saw in the Hi-Ho camp convinced him that there was no design in nature —that she worked regardless of form or plan. The two thousand men who died of cholera were just so much casual waste.

And if the life of the Hi-Ho's was in this manner wasted, then why not his own? Nature was probably going to push him aside in just the same way. He was following the same path as they had followed—one that led to a mass cremation pile.

Wim thought to talk to Doctor Bruin about it, but Bruin was unapproachable. He too had sealed himself away from the horror—had faced it—seen no solution to the problems it had raised, and had shelved it until he had the inspiration to face it again and find some answer.

Wim had to talk to somebody, so he took his anxieties to Schiller, who did not even have to think to reply:

"The ways of God are wonderful; we should not question them. Whatever happens, He knows best. Have faith in Him."

At dawn on the fourth day, an angry dawn, with a sky like the weals on the flesh of a man who has been flogged—the job was done. The clearing where the camp had stood was just so many piles of ashes swept into neat squares at the bidding of the Japanese corporal, and the "Wandel Plug" had climbed into a lorry and been driven back to the landing barge and ultimately to the island.

Wim Peterson went swiftly downhill after that, because he could foresee no future. The Hi-Ho's had been expendable. He was expendable too—waste that was waiting to be incinerated and swept into a neat square pile of ashes.

PART TWO

—

CHAPTER I

THE Koreans who served the Japanese as camp guards were
mostly conscripted peasants with no love for their masters.

On the Japanese side, the Koreans were looked upon as
lazy, unmilitary and untrustworthy. For one Japanese to call
another "a Korean" was the worst possible insult.

Their dislike, therefore, one for the other was mutual and
resulted in quarrels and fights.

It had happened that, that very evening, the "Smiler" had
been waylaid by a group of Japanese when he was returning
to camp and had been badly beaten.

At once those of the guard who were off duty had banded
together and, without permission from the Sergeant, had left
the island in small canoes for the mainland and revenge.

In the darkness it was impossible to make out the shape and
limits of the airfield. Van Reebek, however, knew its lay-out
perfectly. All night long, every night that he worked with the
night shift, he made a slow circuit of it, round and round,
covering its perimeter as many as five times.

His men were scattered in groups, clearing jungle, levelling
the runways and building dispersal bays. At each group he
stopped to talk with the workers, passing on the latest information about the disposition of the Japanese overseers and
guards or the mood of the Sergeant-Major in charge of the
night's work. When he had them, he handed on scraps of news
that he picked up from Malayan or Chinese labourers as he
passed them; news of local affairs mostly, such as the market
price of rice, rumours of a few free white men who worked in
the jungle organising guerilla bands and news of Japanese
troop movements and concentrations. Van Reebek was a
professional soldier. He tried to carry in his mind, always, a
picture of the combat possibilities of the enemy forces in the

neighbourhood. It was very unlikely that the knowledge would ever be useful, but there was always a chance that it might.

The Japanese worked the men on piece-work. They were given a task; when they finished it they could rest; if they did not finish it within the time set, the overseers and the guards came amongst them with sticks and drove them, beating them until the job was done. The work was monotonous, carrying earth, shovelling earth, cutting scrub: those were the only possible variants. The men became apathetic. In that condition Van Reebek knew they were inclined to forget to take precautions against overstepping the rules. They might casually light a cigarette or talk: neither talking nor smoking was permitted except at rest periods. If they broke the rules they were beaten, so it was for their own sakes that he tried to make them observe the orders.

The petrol flares by which they worked threw a hard white light in the immediate vicinity of the gallows from which they were suspended, but it was darkness that predominated, stretching in across the airfield like fog seeping between a few isolated street lamps on the outskirts of a town.

Had they had any will for it, it might have been easy for men to escape. But no one ever tried, for though it might be simple to get away from the guards, there was a price on the head of any escaped white man or Indonesian brought into the Japanese and there were always Malays willing to claim the price. If a man escaped and was caught, he would be killed. If he were not caught, then a hostage would be taken from the camp he had escaped from; usually it was the senior Allied officer, and he would be beaten or killed in the man's stead. So the stakes were too high and there was too little hope of freedom for those who thought of escape.

The men had nothing in their lives to look forward to. Release might come eventually, if the Allied run of victories kept up, but even that hope was becoming a forlorn one, for there were every day new rumours that in the event of an Allied invasion of the area the prisoners were to be driven into already prepared bunkers and annihilated, or sent on marches into the interior from which there would be no return.

Van Reebek tried hard to distract his men, tried to keep them from brooding—but it meant hard work, constant invention of topics that would leave them something fresh to chew over as he passed on. It required, too, a great deal of exertion to keep on the move all night long. At times he was rewarded for his work. because the men came to life for him and he felt he left them warmed and active again when he passed on to the next group.

He was talking now to some men who were carrying basketfuls of earth from a bank and dumping it where a blast wall was being built.

"That Timmers," he was saying, "has just come to me and asked if he could kill some Koreans and some Japanese.

" 'How can you do that,' I asked him, 'over here where there are no Koreans'.

" 'Ah, Lieutenant,' he replied, 'you are wrong. The Koreans are here. I saw them landing from canoes. They are come with sticks. There is to be more fighting between them and the Japanese. When they fight let me get between them with my blade and they will not know who among them has been killing, for my blade is sharp and they will not see me.'

"I wish I could have let him do it," went on Van Reebek, "but he might have made a mistake and allowed himself to be seen. Then those yellow bastards—both kinds of them— would have turned on us, and we are as easy to kill as wood lice. So I had to forbid him. Though I thanked him, for he brought us a warning.

"Beware, all of you, in case any of the fighting occurs around here. If it does, remember it is an affair between husband and wife and it is none of your business. Such wars in the domestic circle are as sacred from interference as is the act of copulation itself. You would not tear a man off his woman—then leave the Japanese with their Koreans." Van Reebek used his crude metaphor deliberately, seeking to wring a little humour of a kind which the men appreciated most out of a situation which might be full of danger. He knew it was very unlikely that any of the men were ignorant of that danger; but there were always those who might think the opportunity offered by a Korean left insensible on the ground too good to be allowed to pass, and would kill the man. While every dead Japanese or Korean was a good one, the repercussions that would follow, if it became known that a prisoner of war was the killer, would be fearful indeed.

Among those men working were several who should have been in camp, sick, but who preferred to work, either because they refused to give in to their sickness, or because by working they were entitled to more food, or because by working voluntarily in the night shift they were making it possible for some friend who was in a worse condition than they were to stay behind and rest. These men Van Reebek singled out for special attention. He went and spoke to each one, encouraging them, making them laugh, perhaps giving them a little tobacco or any other small extra that he might be able to acquire. There was a camp fund for such purchases. The fund had been Van Reebek's idea and it had at once been adopted by the Commandant. Any money left in the possession of a man who died was held and used by the officers in charge of the various working-parties to help those who had the strength of will to keep struggling on. To keep a man's spirit alive in him was more important than physical health. The spirit could carry the body along, though it were almost dead. The body without the spirit wilted rapidly. The Commandant and the doctors encouraged the men to go with the working-parties if they felt they possibly could. By means of the fund they sought to offer stimulation to those who were on the borderline between having the strength of will to force themselves on and those lacking it.

His tour of the men of the party completed, Van Reebek moved on. He had to pass through several hundred yards of darkness before he reached the next group.

It was a darkness full of dread for Van Reebek. Every time he moved off into it there was a chance that he might meet a Japanese and be unable to identify himself. Once, earlier, he had been shot at by a sentry, and he had twice been assaulted by guards who hadn't realised who he was.

When he reached the fringe of a light again he paused, thinking he heard someone call. The sound came from slightly behind him.

"Ss-sst." He turned. In a small earthen bay that had been built to protect a machine-gun post he was able to make out a pale blur that might have been a man's face.

Van Reebek glanced round to see if he had been observed by any of the guard. There were none within sight. He moved across to the gun position.

In the dim light he made out his Chinese friend who was the purveyor of news. They spoke Malay together.

"Big news, Tuan," said the Chinaman. "American bombers

raided Singapore yesterday and sank a Japanese cruiser lying in the Johore Strait."

"Big news, indeed," said Van Reebek. "Is it in your paper?"

"It would never be there. No, my brother who works in the city sent me the information with the driver of a lorry." The man paused and looked round nervously. "Now I must go back to my work," he said. "Here is the paper." He handed Van Reebek the tightly rolled little packet. Then he was gone.

Van Reebek took his time, folding the paper smoothly and evenly, placing it in an inner lining which he had specially sewn into his top pocket.

The newspapers were single foolscap sheets and could be placed there without showing a bulge. Anyone putting a hand into his pocket might perhaps think that the back of the pocket was a little stiff, but would not notice the slit that was part of the pocket flap unless he looked very carefully.

When Van Reebek looked up he was surprised to see another figure in the opening of the gun position. Whoever it was stood still watching him, though in the darkness it would probably have been impossible for the man to have seen what Van Reebek was doing.

The young Dutchman moved nearer to find out who it was. He saw that the man wore the distinctive cap of a Japanese soldier, also that he was carrying a thick stick over his shoulder. Van Reebek saluted and was about to speak when the other made a hushing sound and waved him back into the recess of the gun position. The man followed Van Reebek in and turned, so that a little light fell on his face. Van Reebek saw that it was the Poisoned Frog, one of the Korean guard commanders from the island and the worst and most brutal of all of them.

At the thought that the Korean might have seen him receive a newspaper from the Chinaman, Van Reebek felt a weakening in his stomach.

The Poisoned Frog was very conspiratorial, just as his predecessor the Chinaman had been. Like the Chinaman, he spoke Malay.

Van Reebek was not to make a sound. The Japanese did not know that the Koreans were on the airfield. He, the Poisoned Frog, had come to offer Van Reebek a chance to help the Koreans to punish the Japanese. The prisoners and the Koreans would hunt together. There were only twelve

Japanese on the airfield, there were eighteen Koreans. What Van Reebek must do was to stop any other Japanese coming to the rescue. His men must stop the Japanese from the barracks joining in the fight. He, the Poisoned Frog, made that an order. Did Van Reebek understand?

Van Reebek replied that he understood perfectly but that he could not order his men to do what the Koreans desired.

Why, were they afraid? Weren't the Japanese their enemies?

Van Reebek shook his head. "I cannot order my men to do it," he said emphatically. For a moment he thought the Poisoned Frog was going to hit him. Then the little man— his head came below Van Reebek's chin—turned and disappeared quickly into the darkness. Almost before he had gone a third visitor to the gun position arrived. It was one of the Japanese corporals in charge of the work. Again the conversation was in Malay, only this time the corporal spoke the language very poorly.

"Man? What kind of man?" he pointed in the direction that the Poisoned Frog had taken.

"I see no man," replied Van Reebek.

"What make you here?"

"Pi-pi," said Van Reebek.

"Go," ordered the Japanese. "Go."

As Van Reebek passed him the Japanese kicked his shins. "Go," he repeated, and then muttered a lot more in Japanese which Van Reebek did not understand.

Van Reebek went, moving quickly and with relief into the orbit of the next light, mixing with the men of the next party.

He told them nothing of his encounter with the Poisoned Frog or the corporal. He told them only of the American raid on the Johore Strait and warned them, as he had the others, about the possibility of there being trouble between the Japanese and the Koreans. Inside he was apprehensive: he knew trouble was brewing. Even if his men did not get involved, he was already involved. The Poisoned Frog would never forgive him and would make a personal enemy of him from now on. The corporal too would probably treat him with suspicion and keep him under stricter surveillance, so that his opportunities of contacting the coolie labour to buy tobacco or sugar for the "fund" would be more limited. It was bad luck. And it was more: it made for anxiety and fear, the worst kind of fear, that of knowing that the future held some

99

kind of beastliness without specifying the kind or the extent.

That night the Koreans weakened in their resolve. Instead of a pitched battle with the Japanese as they had intended, they moved away from the airfield and ambushed one Japanese only as he returned down the track from the village to the barracks. They beat him severely, much worse than the "Smiler" had been beaten. They robbed him of all his clothes and left him broken and bleeding in the middle of the dirt on the surface of the track. He subsequently died of his injuries.

Van Reebek knew nothing of this at the time and spent an anxious night waiting for the battle to materialise. Just before dawn the knowledge of the event reached the airfield. A coolie had found the man. He had still been able to speak when he was brought into the barracks.

The news spread among the Japanese on the airfield. They became more taciturn than ever and easily angered. It made things very difficult for the prisoners of war and particularly for Van Reebek.

2

At dawn each day all the men in the camp were mustered on the *midan* in the middle of a square of huts backed by rubber trees. The sun-baked mud at their feet showed smooth and pink, like skin through a hole in a sock. The men were called to attention. They had to bow to the guard commander and then to the rising sun, whilst the guard commander chanted a prayer. After that they were counted and dismissed.

The smoke from the cookhouse rose in a pastel smudge above the trees. The sounds of life in the camp were hushed, so that someone dropping a pan in the cookhouse created a disturbance, like a dissonant chord on brass heard against muted strings.

The clatter seemed to have been the signal which the whole camp had been waiting for, for there began a show of slowly increasing animation.

Men came staggering from the cookhouse carrying between them, two by two, long sticks from which were suspended four-gallon kerosene cans that were filled with "pap", a mixture containing a little rice and a lot of boiling water blended into a thin, milky paste.

In each hut the officer in charge of the hut stood at the head of the queue and superintended the issue of the morning meal. Each man got two mugfuls of pap and a small mugful of milkless, unsweetened tea.

The man who issued the rice in Captain Den Hertog's barrack was a grizzled old sergeant-major who had already been twenty-five years in the Dutch army. Like his captain, who was almost as old and equally grizzled in the military service, Sergeant-Major Slikhuis had learned that self-preservation, though an instinct in every man, is something that reaches its peak only if it is combined with a cunning that is particularly easy to cultivate in the regular armed forces.

In most of the other barracks the officer and his immediate subordinate delegated the menial task of issuing the food to one of the more feeble of the light-duty men. Captain Den Hertog and his sergeant-major had no false pride.

They did not really swindle the men outrageously in the issue of food. It was just that each mugful of rice that was ladled out was not quite full to the top, was, perhaps, a twentieth of an inch short of the brim. With a mug three inches high, sixty rations short by even so minute a quantity meant that there was an extra mugful left at the end. With two hundred and fifty men to serve it meant two extra mugfuls for the captain and two for his sergeant-major—double rations.

Unfortunately for the men, the sergeant-major had it in his power to make life unpleasant for any man who made an official complaint about the issue of rations or any other criticism of the two senior men in the barrack. It was the sergeant-major who drew up the roster for the working-party men. In this he was scrupulously fair and had no favourites— unless there was someone who complained about the issuing of rations. That man would find himself on the list for all the worst jobs.

The sergeant-major was quite open with the men about cheating them of their rations. He justified it by saying that they were able to go out of the camp with the working-parties and not only thereby qualify for bigger rations but also have the opportunity to obtain by barter or otherwise food from the coolies.

When it was suggested that there was nothing to prevent him from giving up his job in the barrack and joining a working-party, and that one of the light-duty men could equally well do the job of keeping rosters, issuing food, superintending the cleaning of the barracks and so on, he at once became sly and smiling and asked if anyone, anywhere, would expect an old soldier to be caught like that. He was a sergeant-major, not a recruit.

Captain Den Hertog agreed entirely with the sergeant-major. He too was not going to be caught.

His billet, which was alongside the sergeant-major's at the end of the long hut that housed his entire company, was screened off with mats from the view of its other occupants and his bed-space was wider than any man's in the camp. Most of the men in his company were young Indonesians who went in awe of his seniority and age. They were used to confined quarters and did not think it worth worrying about that he was depriving those nearest him of several inches of living space. Elsewhere in the other huts it was different; when men are reduced in their circumstances, as were the prisoners of war, the sanctity of small possessions becomes much greater. A nail in the wall, a few inches of bed-space, part of a piece of wire to hang clothes on, these things were as important and as much to be preserved for their owner's use as the privacy of a man's house or his right to build a fence between his garden and the one next door.

There were many bitter arguments between a man and his neighbour in the camps over any encroachment into their bed-space by the latter, even though he came only the width of a finger beyond his own allotted space.

Captain Den Hertog had room enough behind his mat to fit in two more men. In this space with his sergeant-major he used to sit and eat his morning "pap".

To it, as he quite often did, came Doctor DeGoyer. The morning meal was done and the daylight shift had moved off to change places with the night shift as they landed from the barge.

"And Mijnherr," asked Den Hertog, "how is it with you? Have you news?"

DeGoyer nodded. "Singapore had been bombed: it came in with a sick man who was sent back in a rigor from the other side."

"So? That is good. They come nearer."

DeGoyer nodded again. "Ja. It is good." There was satisfaction in his voice.

"There is more too," he went on, as he settled himself with his back against the wall and his feet along the bedding ledge. Den Hertog sat higher up the ledge, cross-legged like a tailor on his bench. The likeness could be carried further, for he was sewing a patch into the sleeve of his green drill uniform jacket.

"More? What more?"

"The Commandant is sinking. He is only lucid now in spells. I have spoken with Bruin and pointed out that someone must be appointed to take his place."

"And what did that Mijnherr say?"

"He agreed that something would have to be done soon."

"So-o? And?"

DeGoyer shrugged. "We must wait and see. But nobody can deny that you are the senior officer in the camp. You would take the job, I suppose?"

"I suppose. I could go sick and direct the camp from my bed the same way that the Englishman does now, couldn't I?"

DeGoyer looked sideways out of the corners of his eyes at his friend.

"That would be one way," he said. "All the privileges without the responsibility. Someone else would have to go and deal with the guard, no?"

"And you would be my doctor?"

DeGoyer laughed.

"Fine," he said. "Fine."

After that there was a long silence.

"One of the men in here sold a watch last night to Mad Harry," said Den Hertog.

"Did he get a good price for it?"

"Slikhuis says it was over two hundred."

"Who was the man?"

"Barnar, one of the half-castes."

DeGoyer scratched his leg and then looked at the dirt he had gathered under his nails.

"Has he made any arrangement about getting anything brought in?"

"Not yet, as far as I know. He is a secretive sort of an individual."

"You mean that whatever he is going to do with the money, he has to keep it from you and old Slikhuis. He must bury his kill to keep it from the vultures."

"You are a fine one to talk of vultures."

DeGoyer was laughing again. Den Hertog and Slikhuis *were* old vultures, dusty looking, baldheaded, somehow faintly benevolent and at the same time to be trusted about as far as the length of a dog's leash.

DeGoyer's laugh came from deep in his chest.

Den Hertog looked at him over the steel-rimmed spectacles he was wearing to see his stitching, turning his head, with the chin down, as he looked at the Doctor first with one eye and then with the other, puzzled by his laughter.

"Ho, ho, ho." DeGoyer caught the look and was convulsed again. The very actions and the long, stringy neck were those of a vulture too.

Then with a sigh he got up.

"I must go and do a round of the hospital barrack. I will see you again soon." He left the hut.

3

Doctor Bruin was seated at the foot of the Commandant's bed-space when Van Reebek came in to report.

Both of the older men listened in silence to all the Lieutenant had to say. The Commandant's eyes were moving restlessly behind their puffed lids and he was obviously taking in what Van Reebek was saying. When the report was done the old man pushed himself a bit more upright.

"Pity about the Poisoned Frog," he said. "He is a sadistic little swine: one among about twenty or thirty men in this camp out of the whole two thousand who have not a single good streak in their make-up. It is good to hear that the Americans have paid Singapore a visit. That will do the men in the camp a lot of good."

Doctor Bruin was watching his patient and thinking: he is brave, this man; he knows he has not much further to go and he is talking as if death was no more than a visit to a friend! And the Doctor wondered, as he had been wondering ever since he first got up, whether the B1 could save the old man's life or whether he was too far gone. So far only he and DeVissar knew that the vitamin concentrate was in the camp. He knew he should really consult one of the other doctors for an opinion, but he felt disinclined to. DeGoyer would not give him an honest opinion and the others all knew of the strong friendship that existed between the Commandant and the Senior Medical Officer and would, out of respect and kindness towards both of them, advise Bruin to make the injection.

Wrapped in these thoughts, Bruin had not been listening to what the Commandant had been saying, and found himself appealed to for confirmation of something the old man had said.

"I do not know what you were talking about; I was not listening."

"Oh, damn you, Jan—have I got to struggle through it again? No, I am hanged if I will. You were too busy day-dreaming to hear my reasons. I said that I thought Van Reebek was the best man to take over my job as Commandant, and that he had better begin tomorrow. Do you agree?"

Bruin frowned, trying even now to grasp what the Commandant was saying.

"Well, do you or don't you?"

"I . . . Don't you think you are being premature?"

"Oh, come, Jan. You are letting some kind of sentimentality mix in where it is better left out."

Bruin heard himself saying slowly, "Yes, yes, I agree. Van Reebek is the best man, but there will be a lot of trouble from certain quarters. He is not the most senior man by far, and young too."

"I have thought all about that and I cannot help it. I mean I cannot help the feelings of others. Van Reedek has the following of the men; he has courage, though I do not imagine he thinks he has; and he will make a job of it. None of the others will."

"Yoshimitsu will not hear of your giving up."

"He will not be difficult. Tell him that I have to have a rest if I am to recover and that I have delegated my job tem-porarily to Van Reebek here."

All this time Van Reebek had stood mute, a dazed look on his face, like a man who has suddenly been told of the death of his parents.

He wanted to turn and run away, to hide. The prospect of being Camp Commandant appalled him. There were men and officers in the camp who were old enough to be his father, men who had been brought up on the patriarchal system still so prevalent in Holland—white men who knew him to be a half-caste.

He stood there shaking his head in negation without knowing that he did it.

Bruin and the Commandant were watching him.

"Sit down, Van Reebek," said the Commandant.

Van Reebek was glad to.

"Just at the moment, my friend," the Commandant said, "you are thinking about yourself. You are afraid for yourself, that the responsibility will be too great, that you will fail, that you will suffer more. You are wrong. You will not fail. I have been watching you. You instinctively take responsibility; I have seen you do it often against your own better judgment. What you imagine to be fear is sensitivity, and that is something you must have if you are to be a leader, and always provided you have something in you which will drive you past it."

The Commandant stopped talking and turned his eyes to Bruin, but without seeing him. He was trying to think of a way to put the necessary resolution into the younger man whom he was about to saddle with what he knew was a testing job.

"Van Reebek," he said at last, "I am not asking you if you will do this, I am ordering you to do it. I am telling you that you are to take over from me as Commandant of this camp and that you will start as from tomorrow. So you need waste no more thought on it. Bruin here will back you up in your difficulties as he has always backed me up. You will need him as I have. There is nothing more to be said now. Except that for a little while I shall be able to help you too. Now go away and sleep. I think highly of you, Van Reebek, as highly as I have ever thought of any man."

For several seconds Van Reebek did not move, then at last he stood up. As he looked at the Commandant there was a suggestion of laughter in his eyes when he said:

"May I wish you a speedy recovery, Kapitan, and a return to the command soon?"

The Commandant nodded approvingly.

"Good boy," he said, and tried to smile too. "Shall you be going out with the working-party again this evening?"

"Yes, Kapitan, I think so."

"Fine."

Van Reebek saluted and turned and left the barrack.

After a moment the Commandant turned to Bruin.

"By the way, that question of the tobacco, Jan. Get as much of it as the men can pay for: if they are going to die, let them die happy, even if they die a little quicker. Don't you agree?"

Bruin nodded gravely. "Yes," he said, "yes." He felt in his heart that he had much to say, but he added only, "I'm glad your answer to the question is something I can agree with."

As he stood up he looked from the Commandant to Wim Peterson, who lay across the gangway, but further down it. Both faces, with the skin stretched over the sodden tissues, were without wrinkles, both lay without movement: but one was seventeen and the other—old, with many full years behind him.

CHAPTER II

"HIGH against the sky stood the image of an enormous, snarling black face, supported at a height of forty feet on elaborate scaffolding. From between the writhing lips a great tongue uncurled at a steep slope to the ground. An ornate stairway wound round the structure, terminating in a small room within the head. In the days before the Japanese brought the war to Java, honey coloured men and their children had carried mats up the stairs and, perching themselves on them, had shot laughing out of the mouth and down the curling tongue to the ground.

"Now, the small room in the head was a Japanese sentry-post. Through apertures in the effigy's eyes, ears and the ornate collar the man on duty had a view of the entire camp spread out among the booths and stalls of what had once been a fair-ground and was now populated by prisoners of war."

Doctor Bruin was again reading the book the Commandant had given him.

"I was happy to come to that camp," the old man had written, "and came to it straight from hell. We had been working on the Outer Islands, officers and men, levelling a coral reef as an airstrip. The Japanese had worked us fourteen hours a day on our hands and knees, with hammers, chipping the coral to make it smooth. During the day the sun pressed down on the backs of our necks and its rays were reflected up off the coral so that it struck into our eyes with needles of white fire. At night the flickering light of the flares made the coral blink and produce a sort of madness in the men which resulted in something like epilepsy. Many of them went blind. Even then the Japanese did not relent, but kept them working, feeling for the coral nobs with their bare hands. When they found a nob they had to strike sightless at it with their hammers until it was gone.

"We were within reconnaissance range of Allied aircraft bases in New Guinea. When British or American aircraft came over I saw men weeping because they knew that in an hour or two the pilots and crews of the flying machines above their heads would be back in a world that was friendly and familiar, where, though they were operating from jungle bases, they had milk in their tea and the easy companionship of free men.

"The journey we made back from the Islands was another kind of hell. We were battened in the lower holds of a cargo ship, with a dysentery epidemic, only one latrine bucket per hundred men and no medical attention. All the doctors, who had no drugs anyway, were battened down together in another hold and not permitted to visit around the ship.

"Our food and water were lowered to us on the same rope that was used to haul the latrine bucket up and was in buckets too; one bucket of fresh water per twenty men per day, one of rice swill.

"The death-rate was high and the dead stayed with us to the end. Some of the bodies lay among us for a week. In the stifling heat of the holds the flesh putrified quickly.

"So the fair-ground camp in the highlands of Java, when we reached it, was so strange that it was like being released unexpectedly from an underground cave into a world full of sunlight and fields of spring flowers.

"None of us could believe our senses when we first got there. Sight, sound, smell—all were reborn. The prisoners who were already in the fair-ground camp were all healthy and vigorous. There was plenty of food, even restaurants, where sweet coffee, meat dishes and bread could be bought. Everywhere the buildings were still bright, even garish, with coloured paints. There were orchestras playing, a theatre, a library. There were two football fields and the men were fit enough to play on them.

"Except for the sentry in the shute-the-shute tower, we never saw a guard.

"I can think of nothing to compare with the sense of release we found in that place. Even when the end comes and we walk out free men we shall not experience a greater peace than we did for the first few days at the fair-ground camp. It saved our lives and our wits.

"No one there was forced to work outside the camp, though a few men did go out voluntarily to work on vegetable farms. Within the camp there were well-organised parties of men who kept it clean, and, operated entirely by the prisoners of their own initiative, there were a soap factory, a pencil factory, a bakery, a mill that made rice-paper and a properly equipped hospital.

"Why were all these things in this one camp that existed nowhere else? I don't know. The Japanese officer in charge was a smiling little man who, I think, liked to be able to play Santa Claus; but he must have been operating on orders received from higher up, for all the officers and men in the camp were paid weekly, and fairly liberally, whether they worked or not. One thing that did have some bearing on the question was that at that time Japan was still apparently winning the war.

"For weeks I lived in the warmth of recovering sanity and health. My body, which had reached its last resources, began to build up reserves again. My mind, which sought frantically for diversion, found it.

"Later, much later, when I felt strong enough, I turned about and faced backwards down those months in the Outer Islands.

"After the first six weeks on the coral my mind had become paralysed. It received impressions, but could not transfer them into thought or into any relationship with the surroundings or conditions of existence. After we got to the fairground camp I kept my memories hidden, and when I took them out it was cautiously as an old maiden lady might now and then take a sip of the alcohol that drove her father to ruin.

"Then one day I received a jolt that brought me savagely back face to face with the Japanese and the meaning of captivity.

"Nine coloured men from Menado—some of the Dutch coloured troops imprisoned with us—got out of the camp and went to meet some women with whom they had in some mysterious way been in contact. They were betrayed by the Javanese outside the wire, brought back into the camp and executed.

"We were forced to witness the execution. Ranged in a wide horseshoe round one of the football fields, the whole camp watched the firing squad, which had been drawn from the camp guards, do its work. There were eighteen riflemen and they fired ten volleys before their victims were all finally dead.

"The Menadonese were tied, naked, by one foot, to a stake

in the ground so that they could not run away. Some of them were hideously and pitifully wounded before they finally ceased to move. Because they were naked, each time they were hit the full nature of the injury was visible. They jerked and twitched, almost jumping at the impact of the bullets. A man stood with a broken bone thrust through torn skin and blood pumping evenly from a severed artery. Another, with a shattered pubis, stood looking down in horror and agony, stooped forward, almost double, like a collapsed golliwog, until another bullet struck the crown of his head, shattering it like a lamp bulb.

"The firing squad were issued with only one round at a time, so that there was a long pause between each volley. The execution took nearly twenty minutes from the first shot to the last.

"It was suggested afterwards by some of the men in the camp that the Japanese had deliberately ordered their men to shoot as badly as they had done in order to make the scene more terrifying for the spectators. I believe that the men who held the rifles were just appalling marksmen who grew more and more unnerved by their own inept efforts to kill the men in front of them.

"When all nine men were finally dead their bodies were put in coffins which had stood nearby all the time. There followed a military funeral, with full honours. Before the cortège moved off the smiling Japanese Commandant, solemn for this occasion, stood with his hat off before the line of coffins and, bowing to each one, addressed it in Japanese.

"The dead men, leaving despite their coffins a trail of blood through the camp, were then carried to graves that had been dug for them in a circle round the shute-the-shute tower.

"The execution took place at dawn. It was noon before we fell out from the funeral parade and returned to our billets. When I reached mine I was shaking and had to lie down.

"I hoped that resting on my bed would bring some sort of relief from the agitation and fever that I felt in my blood and bones. They increased. I was sweating with the effort to thrust the whole episode behind me so that I could rest for a few moments, but the greater the effort I made the more insistent became the morbid urge to go over the whole desperate scene again.

"In the end I gave in. For a few terrible moments I went

through a physical and mental orgasm that left me afterwards wonderfully supine and clear-headed.

"Through the evening and through the night I lay in my bunk without moving. Like a fisherman checking over a long stop-net that is in need of repair, I worked back over the experiences that had made me into the man I was.

"Religion failed me in adolescence. For a long time after that failure I paid lip-service to a belief in Christianity because I knew nothing else and because I was afraid to hurt those about me, who might find me criminal for breaking with the Faith they had tried to foster in me. Then came a stage of nothingness. It was followed by an increasing belief in atheism.

"As an atheist, I knew that I was a compound of chemical substances imbued with some as yet unspecified force that made me animate. In normal death the worn-out chemicals would return to an inanimate state: I would cease to be, and that was the end of that.

"But now the death of the Menadonese made me think again.

"They died purposelessly and hideously. They died, being young and unmarried, except for the 'ashes to ashes and dust to dust' aspect, probably without issue.

"I too am without issue and I am old.

"I am to leave nothing. My life has been for nothing.

"If I were a good atheist, I should accept that. But even atheism has failed me. I must believe that I can make something of myself and leave something of myself.

"Again, the hideous deaths of the Menadonese have convinced me that whatever I make of myself, it must not be something that is brutal and causes unnecessary suffering. I must remember that my mind is as sensitive as my body. I feel with my mind and I must do nothing to cause it pain, or to cause pain to the minds of others. I must make something of myself, and leave something of myself, and both things in such a way that I will cause no pain to others.

"In this I believe I have found a fundamental truth—not an original one, but one which I have arrived at through my own suffering and endeavour. The best thing I can do is to try to show this truth to others, and the best way to show it is through my own example.

"Here in prison camp I tried first to escape my destiny; then I tried to strike back at it by downing others in my battle for survival; now I have made my peace with it, and can face it squarely and say, 'I know you and I am no longer afraid of you; we must work together and then perhaps I can temper some of your mercilessness'."

Doctor Bruin put the book down. For a moment or two he lay still. A mosquito whined round his head, then went away. Moments later he felt a slight prick on his right hand and absently struck at it with the other. Then he rolled over on his side and, glancing across to Smith to see if he was still reading, saw that he was laying with his eyes shut. So the Doctor turned down the wick in the hurricane lamp and blew it out.

He didn't sleep for several hours. When he did eventually go off he had decided that he would give the vitamin concentrate to Wim Peterson and another of the younger men, after he had checked with DeGoyer to see if he agreed that they were the most likely to benefit from the injection.

2

Smith was not asleep when Bruin put his light out. He was finding it increasingly difficult to sleep at nights.

If he had been able to do a little more during the day, he might have been tired enough to sleep, but there was so little he could do. With a few exceptions, the men in the barracks did not want to hear about God. Smith was not imaginative enough to talk to them about much else. His experience of life and the world outside the ministry was very limited. Though he had been a number of years in Africa, it had always been an alien land. He had never tried to think himself into the lives of the black people. Their ways to him were incomprehensible and evil and must be changed to his before he could meet them on any common ground. They worshipped spirits that were represented by trees and thunder and other natural phenomena, not a spirit that was represented by a figure on a cross. Their mythology was only known to them by word of mouth and had not achieved the clear comprehensibility of print. So he had learned nothing of Africa but had tried instead with all his might to teach those who came to the Mission that among other things it was wicked to whistle on Sundays and wicked to go naked in the hot sun.

In the prison camps, though he could hold no services, he had tried to teach people about God as he had been taught about Him himself. He went to them individually, those who could speak English, and told them of the 'redemption of sins', of 'the life everlasting', of 'the mercy of God'. Some were actually rude to him, others politely bored, a few prepared to listen and argue. He preferred the latter, for he felt that if he could only argue back with some inspiration he might save them.

But all the time it was obvious that the tendency of those who were suffering was to turn from God rather than towards Him. To Smith this had seemed inexplicable. Suffering, he had always thought, should have brought people nearer to God rather than further away from Him. Even in death there were quite a number who spurned angrily the offer of salvation.

Only the Catholic priests held most of their adherents steady. There had been a Jesuit Father, an English-speaking Dutchman, in one camp who gave away part of his scant food to others and who invited the scornful to argue with him in full debate in public. An exhibitionist, Smith had thought him a sort of Christian fakir. But he had held his co-religionists to their creed and had even made one or two conversions. Laughingly he had replied to Smith one day when the latter had been commenting on the Father's successes:

"Oh, ja, Mijnheer but you, you offer only bread and water, we offer an iced cake glittering with candles. Even a starving man knows which to choose."

It had shocked Smith to hear the man speak so cynically. He had always thought of the Catholic Church as being the most sentimental and that it was his own that was realist and, in offering bread rather than cake, more likely to appeal to those who faced the realities.

But here in prison, as the Catholic Father had said, starving men preferred cake to bread when they were capable of believing in the promise of either.

And now he himself was well down the road to unbelief, to wondering whether the fulfilment of the promise did not seem to be remote and uncertain.

Smith, hearing Bruin sigh in the darkness, asked:

"Doctor, do you believe that faith can cure sickness?"

There was a long silence. Eventually Bruin replied, "Faith is a peculiar thing in my experience. In medicine, when faith can feed on tangible facts, or a report of some tangible fact that the patient finds reasonable, then it can do wonders, far more than any drug."

Smith did not feel that he quite understood what the Doctor meant, but was afraid to press his query further because he could see that Bruin had turned on his side away from him as if his answer had been final and he didn't want to say any more.

PART THREE

—

December 25th, 1944
Christmas Day

CHAPTER I

CHRISTMAS DAY dawned quietly: the air was still and leaden with the threat of heat to come. The smoke from the cookhouse fires smudged low and hung in the tops of the rubber-trees.

The morning was just like any other morning. Yet nearly all the men in the camp, the sick and the day shift, opened their eyes with a sense of expectancy, as if there was to be a change in their affairs. The camp woke to reluctant movement, early, but slowly.

There were no quick, light footsteps as one hears in the early mornings in the streets of Europe. There was nothing brisk in the awakening of the worn-out, hungry men.

The crew of the night shift in the cookhouse stirred the boiling rice 'pap' and made ready to serve it into tins. Before the heat of the fires the men wore nothing but loin-cloths and the sweat made dirty streaks where it ran freely down the backs of those with white skins.

Immediately after he had eaten his breakfast, Doctor Bruin walked across to the hospital barrack.

He found DeGoyer was there before him, and he arrived in time to witness his fellow doctor put on a display that raised his reputation with most of the sick men in his care and brought even lower the opinion Bruin had of him.

Doctor DeGoyer was applying a form of shock treatment to one of his patients, who was to have injected into his veins a small quantity of blood that belonged to a different blood groop to his own.

DeGoyer was himself the blood donor. With a hypodermic syringe he drew a little blood from a vein in his arm and then pricked it into the bloodstream of his patient.

The pantomime that went with the operation lost nothing in the sweep and flourish of Doctor DeGoyer's movements. All eyes were upon him as he withdrew the hypodermic needle from his own arm with a theatrical flourish. He held the syringe aloft to check that it contained the right quantity of blood, holding it in such a way that all could see the blood that the Doctor had given so bravely from his own body.

Then with a deft, quick jab he inserted the needle in the arm of the man who lay before him. Even the expression on his face reflected the drama that he was playing. A fixed gleaming stare and an out-thrust bottom lip.

Bruin shook his head and went and sat at the foot of the Commandant's bed-space. The old man was lying very still with his eyes closed. Doctor Bruin did not disturb him, or speak to him, but laid his hand gently on the Commandant's ankle. It was almost a gesture of pity. The Commandant opened his eyes slowly.

"Well, Jan?" he said.

Bruin smiled.

"How are you?" he asked.

The Commandant closed his eyes again.

"Heavy and tired of this flesh. I am weighted down everywhere with little bags of lead pellets. I feel petulant and as if I want to cry."

Doctor Bruin patted the ankle, but found that he could not say anything.

"I have condemned you to die," he thought, looking at the puffy, grotesque face, "and you are my friend." Then he brought himself up by telling himself that he was indulging in the kind of cheap dramatics that he might expect of DeGoyer. The Commandant would die shortly anyway, the B1 had arrived too late, even if it was given to him: though there was always the gambler's chance that it might pull him round if his will to live were strong enough.

Bruin asked himself for the hundredth time, "Have I any right to take a gambler's chance when the stuff could certainly save two others?"

There was no real hesitation in the Doctor's mind; he had gone over every aspect of the question since he had woken at five that morning.

He gave the Commandant's ankle a final pat and got up.

DeGoyer had finished his act.

Bruin walked down the barracks towards him.

The Commandant opened his eyes again and watched him go. The restraint in the Doctor's bearing had been evident, and the Commandant wondered without any particular anxiety what had caused it.

Bruin bent and looked at the patient whom DeGoyer had been treating; then they both moved on down the hut to the further end, where a narrow corner was screened off. It was Schiller's bed-space and was used, as well, as the repository for the few bottles of drugs that were kept in the hospital. It also served as the barrack office and the general place for consultations between doctors.

The two doctors sat down.

Bruin was silent, staring at the strap of his wooden sandals for several seconds before he spoke.

"Which two of the more critical cases," he asked at length, "have the best chance of recovery if we could get then some B1?"

"Why? Have you got some?"

"Enough for two men."

"I will look round and let you know."

"No." Doctor Bruin wanted no evasions, wanted to avoid giving DeGoyer an opportunity to favour any of the men. He wanted an answer. "I am sure if you think a moment you can tell me now. How about young Peterson?"

"Yes." The word was brought out reluctantly. "I suppose his case is not hopeless. He might get better."

"And another?"

"Let us go and look at Ebens; I should think he would get better too."

"Ebens? Ebens? Oh yes, I remember. All right, Ebens and Peterson. Schiller!" Bruin called the orderly. Though they had decided upon the names, he still did not trust DeGoyer not to change his mind and give the stuff to some friend of his.

As Schiller came up Doctor Bruin said:

"I have a little B1. Enough to put two men on their feet again. Doctor DeGoyer and I have decided that it shall be given to Ebens and Peterson. Here is the stuff. Doctor De-Goyer will arrange with you when he will give the injections."

Schiller did not put out his hand to take the vials.

"But, Mijnheer Doktor," he exclaimed, "what about the Commandant?"

Bruin looked Schiller steadily in the eyes.

"I am afraid it is too late for him," he said. "The chances

are against the stuff being any good to him. Here."

Schiller looked very unhappy.

Bruin shrugged. "It is no good being upset," he said angrily. "It is all quite straightforward. Now take these things and get on with your duty. Doctor DeGoyer will call you when he wants you."

Mutely Schiller took the vials and placed them in a little box which he first unlocked and then locked again afterwards.

When he had gone back up the barrack, DeGoyer said:

"The Commandant is your friend and there is a slight chance that he would pull round."

Bruin felt sick. He took his glasses off and rubbed his eyes.

"No," he said. "It must be Peterson and Ebens." He got up. "We shall be able to see a big difference in them by this time tomorrow."

When he left the barrack he avoided passing the Commandant's bed-space by turning out of a side door.

2

The night shift of the working-party was kept late over on the mainland by the whim of the Japanese sergeant in charge of the work. He announced to Van Reebek that he would accompany the men off to the island in the landing barge and gave orders that they were not to leave without him. He kept eighty men waiting for a full hour while he went back to his billet for his morning food.

The men of the night shift, and Van Reebek too, were tired, hungry and irritable. To struggle all night and then to be kept from their meagre food and rest tried their pitiful strength too far.

Van Reebek was so preoccupied with his irritation, and also with his unease over having to take on the post of Camp Commandant, that he forgot to feel the usual anxiety about getting his men past the guard-house when eventually they were brought over.

It had not occurred to him that, owing to the working-party being late, the guard would have changed and that the guard commander who had passed them out, a reasonable sort of man, would not still be on duty to see them in.

So when they landed it was without much thought that he

fell the men in as usual and waited for someone to come out of the guard-house to count and examine them.

It was with a shock that he saw that the man who came was the Poisoned Frog—a shock from which he quickly recovered. He faced up, at once, to the certainty that there was going to be trouble.

The Poisoned Frog did not look at him or even return his salute, but walked with steady purpose into the ranks of the men and started to examine them individually with great thoroughness. Each one in turn had to step out of his sandals or boots, take off his loin-cloth or his shorts, hand over his hat for careful scrutiny.

It was Timmers whom the Poisoned Frog found carrying on his head, beneath his hat, a small, flat flask of native brandy.

He hauled the little Indonesian out in front of the ranks and, without troubling to call the interpreter, launched into a harangue in Japanese.

Presently there came the first slap across the culprit's face. Then another. Timmers, whose fear of corporal punishment was great, began to tremble and cry.

With a curious detachment and a feeling of the inevitability of it all, Van Reebek stepped forward and forced himself between the Poisoned Frog and Timmers.

The Poisoned Frog moved back a pace or two and looked up into Van Reebek's face. In the little man's eyes there was a look of contemptuous amusement.

The occasion was following exactly the plan he had laid down for it. He knew that Van Reebek too was also aware that it was a set piece.

Van Reebek had crossed him out on the airfield; now he was going to pay for it.

The sergeant from the airfield lit a cigarette, and while he kept apart from the group of guards who had come out of the guard-house to enjoy the sport, he wanted to see how the affair would go.

Unarmed and unable to protect himself in any way, Van Reebek was in the ring to fight his hopeless duel against a man who could hit him at will with anything he liked.

It was as if the Poisoned Frog had issued a challenge to this unequal battle and Van Reebek had accepted it.

The Poisoned Frog took off his heavy leather belt with its

two cartridge pouches and casually flicked the buckle across Van Reebek's face.

Van Reebek felt he was going to flinch but braced himself in time.

The Poisoned Frog took his bayonet out of its scabbard and stuck it in the middle of the circle of his belt which he had dropped on the ground. Then he took the scabbard out of its frog. It was solid leather, tipped with metal, but flexible.

Van Reebek took a deep breath and thanked God that there was a limit to the amount of pain that can be borne and prayed that he would reach that limit quickly; for after that it was all the same, a numb paralysis of the mind, and all that was required was the strength to remain upright until complete and merciful insensibility overtook him.

The Poisoned Frog knew about the limit of pain too and was careful to avoid reaching it quickly.

He flogged Van Reebek about the head and shoulders with the scabbard with great skill, avoiding injury to his victim's eyes but drawing blood from every other part of his face.

The American, Burns, stood with the others from the cookhouse to watch the spectacle. He had been there from the beginning.

With everyone else, he knew that Van Reebek, by deliberately pushing his body between Timmers and the Korean, had laid himself open to the charge of using physical aggression against the guards—something that the Japanese Command would not tolerate—and that he had courted the punishment they saw him taking. He had done it to save a half-wit from taking the beating which he had invited by trying to smuggle liquor into the camp. Burns felt strongly a sense of affinity with the tall young Dutch half-caste who, even after half an hour of punishment, bloodied and with the skin on his face torn and purple from the blows it had received, stood impassively taking it without expression. To Burns, Van Reebek's gesture was a crystallisation of his own sense of the heroic. It was something he had looked for everywhere in the camp and had seen only in the old Commandant.

While the beating was going on Jansen made the mistake of crossing to the guard-house with some food the guards had asked him to prepare for them.

Timmers saw him walk into the guard-house, speak with one of the men there and walk back. The little man was filled suddenly with a great hate for the chief cook. In his confused mind things got mixed up and he saw Jansen as the cause of all his misery. He, Timmers, had to run the risk of a beating to get half a pint of liquor into the camp. Jansen could get it any day from the guards themselves, because he toadied to them.

Van Reebek, Timmers' favourite officer, who had always taken such pains on his behalf, was now suffering not for his, Timmers' sake, but because Jansen was fat and loathsome and crawled to the Japanese sergeant.

A bladder seemed to burst in the half-caste's brain and blood drenched his sight. He saw Jansen through a film of it.

Van Reebek was still on his feet when the Poisoned Frog grew tired of his exercise and dismissed him and the men.

In his excitement the Poisoned Frog had forgotten to take Timmers' bottle of brandy from him.

Timmers took it to the hospital barrack where a Doctor was bathing Van Reebek's wounds and saw to it personally that his lieutenant drank a good tot of it, and left behind enough for another good tot so that Van Reebek should sleep well that afternoon.

As he walked back to his billet, Timmers had to steady himself and fight off his inclination to do violence to Jansen at once. He was aware that he would have to be careful and plan his action so that Jansen's death would not be too obviously a case of murder.

3

A dozen times that morning Schiller looked at the box which contained the vials of B1. He tried hard for a moment or two to keep his feelings back and to judge what he called to himself "the Commandant's case" without personal bias.

Because he had not spared himself in working for the men in the camp, the Commandant had worn himself out. For this reason, a man like Ebens, who had never done a hand's turn for anyone, and was therefore stronger, was to be given preference when it came to the point of trying to save their lives.

Peterson, Schiller could understand. If there were to be two to get the injections, then it was all right that Peterson

should be one of them. But Ebens: and not the Commandant?
It was most unjust.

Then he forgot all about bias and thought only of the
Commandant as a man whom he loved.

Without recognising that his own desires, his own will in
the matter, would provide the answer, he prayed to God for
guidance. At once he felt inspired to do what he could to save
the old man.

Moving backwards and forwards between his patients,
even while closing the eyelids of a man just dead, he thought
over the problem.

By the time the midday rice came round he had decided how
to go about it. After he had served the food to all the others,
he retired to his sheltered corner behind its screen with his
own bowl of thin vegetable stew and rice.

Making sure that no one could overlook him, he took up
the box and deliberately forced the lock. He took out one vial
of B1, closed the box and returned it to its place on the shelf.

He put the vial he had taken inside his shirt so that it rested
against his skin at the waistband of his shorts. Then he got up
to take his bowl out to wash it, thinking to be able to hide
the vial in a hollow tree on his way to the sea.

He found someone sitting by the tree.

He returned to the barrack and anxiously tried to think of
somewhere else to hide it. It must not be anywhere near his
own bed-space. for if Doctor Bruin were to suspect that he
had stolen it then it would be there that he would search.

Presently he got what he thought was a wonderful idea.

He had been too busy during the morning to give the
Commandant his bath. He went to him now with water and
soap. After he had bathed him and on the pretext of looking
for another piece of soap, he opened the Commandant's
rucksack and slipped the B1 into it, rolling it neatly in an old
shirt that lay almost at the bottom of the bag.

Schiller planned to come after lights out, when he was at
liberty to move about the barrack on his own, retrieve the
B1 and give it as an injection to the Commandant.

He could quite easily explain to the old man if he should
ask that it was something that Doctor Bruin had ordered to
be given him.

Schiller guessed rightly that Doctor Bruin would not tell
the Commandant that there was B1 in the camp.

Having concealed the drug where no one would think of looking for it, Schiller went to the Doctor's quarters and reported that his box had been broken into and one vial of the drug stolen.

4

In the course of several moves from one prison camp to another the Catholic Father in the camp had discarded all his possessions so as to be able to carry his cape, stole and other vestments with him. In the last move the Japanese had allowed each man to carry with him only what he could get into a rucksack.

As the Christmas service opened Smith eyed the Father with distaste. Smith wore his only shirt and a pair of shorts, washed and pressed with care between two boards especially for the occasion.

None the less, he felt that dressed as he was he was more suitably clad to appear before God than the man in his garish array of gold and brilliant colours.

There was no doubt that in those surroundings the Catholic priest looked rather out of place, like a brilliant tropical fish that had got into the same pail as a catch of uncooked prawns.

The service was being held in a natural depression in the ground that bordered the bathing beach. An altar had been made out of a packing case and a simple wooden cross had been built by one of the men in the camp out of wood from a rubber-tree.

In the late morning sunlight, and despite the heat, the simple ceremony was carried out with a quiet dignity that was restful and fortifying to the two or three hundred men attending it.

Yoshimitsu had evidently issued orders that the Koreans should not show themselves near the spot where the service was being held; but he himself stood at a considerable distance from it, in the doorway of his hut, to see that there was no incitement to mutiny or any other form of subversion. He had with him DeVissar, who was to explain and translate the ritual and the prayers.

After prayers had been offered by the Protestant and the Catholic priests and a hymn had been sung, Smith moved forward to read the lesson.

He held his Bible lightly in the palm of his hand. He sought, as he read, to inspire the words with the emotion and elation that he felt to be fitting for the moment.

He started quietly:

" 'And it came to pass in those days that there went out a decree from Caesar Augustus . . .' "

With a rising tone he read:

" 'And she brought forth her firstborn son, and wrapped him in swaddling clothes and laid him in a manger; because there was no room for them in the inn.' "

Then he read of the timid shepherds and the angel's call to them and finished with a flourish on the words:

" '—praising God, and saying.

Glory be to God in the highest and on earth peace, good-will toward men.' "

As he spoke the last words without looking at his Bible, Smith, head erect, stood rigid, waiting for the fanfare and cries of joy that he had always felt should greet that great announcement.

And suddenly he was aware that his attitude was a pose: that the words as they echoed away from him in a long perspective meant nothing to him. He felt as if he were dry and had been shrivelled in a hot wind, that he was suddenly light and brittle and useless.

With head bent forward, he walked blindly from his place before the altar and back to the edge of the congregation.

The moment the service was over he went straight to his billet and threw himself face downwards on his bedding mat.

He was so full of despair that he too, like Van Reebek, had reached the peak of suffering and knew pain no more, but only a vast limbo in which he sailed as idle and useless as a piece of straw.

CHAPTER II

LATER that afternoon Timmers was preparing a new song. In his mind, as he sang it over to himself, it went like this.

"The wind is my messenger, it brings to me news of many things. Sometimes it comes lightly, then I know its tidings are good, for good news is easily borne. But times it comes heavily, then I know that it is laden with an evil smell, a smell that might be poison.

"Fat men when they are bad smell bad, smell rancid like rotten oil.

"Such a wind came to me one day and I beheld a thing that brought misery to many. It was a man with a foul crutch and long yellow teeth behind lips like soft cigars. His hand was heavy, moist and thick, and it lay like the heat of boiled flesh across the lives of all those who were about him.

"This man fathered many little creatures that would run from his body at his bidding and they came back to him, fattened on the sweat of others over whom they had run. Then he would eat them and give birth to more again and the process was endless!

"So that while those about him grew to less than threads, the fat one grew as the dead swell when they lie in the sun.

"This one was a man who served three masters, himself, those whom he worked for, and his friends. His little creatures worked for them too. Like white worms of decay they fed off those who lay still, off those who were neither friends nor masters.

"For many ages I saw this man and knew him not. Then I knew him. Then I knew that he was bad and must join the others who had been bad too.

"It was the afternoon of the same day that first I knew him that I went to find him.

"As I left my hall the wind came and blew the dust a little before my feet, playing and gamboling at my feet like a young dog eager to go with his master on a mission and pleased with the prospect of it.

"The tall trees acquiesced too. They bowed their heads and said: 'We are with you, call on us.'

"Among the trees it was very dark and they led me secretly, passing me one to the other.

"The light of the afternoon sun winked on the ground before me, winked, saying: 'Little brother, I see and I do not see. I watch and I do not watch. I shall know and I shall not know.'

"In the heat of that afternoon most men slept and I could smell the rancid one before I saw him.

"He was not in his house and that was good, for there were others there.

"Then I saw him with the yellow one.

"Between them were sacks of rice and the little room they were in was dark.

"I lay with my friend a bush, lay close with her.

"Then came the yellow one away and left the fat one.

"I watched him.

"He thought he was unseen.

"First, because of the heat of the time he took off his clothes, all save the cloth that passed between his legs. And brothers, he was fat. Not as I am fat, a small man with a round, tight pod before him—but fat so that his breasts were as a woman's, cupped and pointed. And his belly hung over his loins in the backward curve of a squatting man. And his head sat on his neck and the flesh fell roll upon roll one over another.

"Then he looked out to see if he could see me, but the bush held me closer to her and he saw me not.

"He turned about then and closed the door. But my bush had a sister that grew beside the house and I crept to her and she too opened her arms to me. From there I could watch the inside through slits in the matting walls.

"There in an unspilled light sat the fat one eating his little people while the folds of his flesh ran grease, ran so that he sat in a pool of it. And when he had finished eating, and he ate much and in a long while, he laid on his face on the sacks to sleep.

"My bush held me quietly. The fat one slept, his feet stretched to me and the great twin mounds of his buttocks fell apart in his sleep and the cloth fell between them.

"Then I took myself to the door and made myself very thin. I went sideways through the small opening of the door and the smell inside was rancid.

"For a moment there was excitement in all that shining flesh. It was as if I suddenly knew a fat woman instead of a fat man. It seemed sweet to me and the skin was rare and fine and the cloth fell between her buttocks.

"After she was dead, she smelt no more and the skin was still rare and fine. Then I dried the body with the cloth I took from between the legs.

"That flesh calls me back even now, but I shall not go, for it was no woman, but a fat, evil thing that had wronged many.

"A fat, dead thing, fat and dead with the flesh spilled over all about it on the sacks of rice, with the buttocks hanging apart and the fat spread out about it like bread dough that has dropped on a hard floor, hugging the floor close."

"Brothers, the fat one is dead."

Timmers sat up and said those last words aloud.

A neighbour looked surprised and answered him:

"You are telling us something we have known this past hour. Something you would have known yourself if you had not been lying there sleeping. He was found dead in the rice store. The doctors say he died of a failure of the heart."

Timmers laughed.

2

Doctor Bruin was sitting by Van Reebek. The latter was lying now in the bed-space between Bruin's and Smith's that had originally been the Commandant's. Bruin had had him brought there after his wounds had been dressed in the hospital barrack. The young lieutenant had slept soundly and had woken in the early evening, with his face and shoulders full of pain but not unbearably so.

He knew that he had done well to take the beating as he had done and that he had started his first day as Camp Commandant auspiciously.

He had only just awakened and Doctor Bruin was bathing one or two open wounds, grazes and abrasions on his face.

They talked for a moment of the beating and then Bruin said:

"While you slept the camp has moved on quite a way." He paused. "Timmers has killed Jansen."

"No! Never! Oh, God, more trouble." Van Reebek was already trying to struggle to his feet.

Bruin smiled and shook his head.

"No," he said, "there will be no trouble. I have taken care of it."

Van Reebek looked at the Doctor in amazement. He was so cool. He was a man at the peak of a performance, keyed to meet all crises without emotion or fault. Also he was already at work on Van Reebek, gaining his confidence, working to promote the understanding they must have between them if they were to run the camp together as successfully as the Doctor and the dying Camp Commandant had done.

Van Reebek relaxed. He knew at once that if Bruin said he had taken care of the trouble then all would be well.

"Tell me about it, Doc."

Bruin stuck a dressing on a wound that was a deep slit between the side of Van Reebek's head and his ear, an adhesive dressing made adhesive by the use of crude latex from a rubber-tree, and replied:

"About an hour and a half ago someone in the cookhouse missed Jansen. They looked for him and found him in the rice store, lying naked on the sacks and quite dead.

"They sent for me. I got there and found that American, Burns, in charge. He had kept his head. Fortunately, he was the first one who was told about it by the man who actually found the body. Burns went straight down to look at it, saw that the man had been murdered, shut the door and turned the key in the lock before anyone else could get there. He kept the key until I arrived. He took me to one side and said, 'Some guy has been in there and knifed him. Neat job too. We must keep it from the Japs. I thought, Doc, maybe it would be better for all concerned if we could make out that he died from heart failure or something.'

"For the moment I thought he might have done it himself and was trying to cover it up. Anyway, no good purpose could be served by letting all the cookhouse in to see the body. Obviously the less excitement there was about it the better, so I got someone to keep the others out and went in with Burns.

"Jansen had been knifed and, as Burns had said, it was a neat job.

"The wound was a slit no more than two centimetres long, and the knife that made it had been placed with a very exact knowledge of anatomy. Jansen carries so much fat that the lips of the wound had closed together and there was no more than a tiny bead of blood. It had already been cleaned once with Jansen's loin-cloth, which lay on the floor. The knife had been cleaned on it too.

"There was an odd feature about the knifing. A long, thin slit had been made with what must have been the tip of a sharp knife right down the spine from the atlas vertebrae and round between the legs. It was little more than a scratch— at various points along the line there were slight scratches running across the body at right angles to the spine. The purpose of the scratches puzzled me for a while and then I saw that they divided the body into the same joints as a butcher divides the carcase of an ox. It seemed to me then that whoever had killed the man must have been crazy. Having plugged the wound and, with Burns' help, having dressed the body again, I announced that death was due to heart failure. Then I made some discreet enquiries about Timmers.

"He was away from his billet for much of the afternoon. He was seen slinking down through the trees towards the cookhouse, and his neighbours in the billet say that he is in an odd, exalted frame of mind now. I have not seen him yet; I thought I would wait until you woke and than send for him and we would interview him together."

"Fine," said Van Reebek. "Have someone fetch him."

When Timmers came in, he came coyly, like a girl in early puberty, and stood looking down, his fingers clapsed in front of his loin-cloth. His amber skin was very sleek and had a dull lustre almost as if it had been oiled. He exuded an aura that was like that of a sleepy, satisfied woman.

Van Reebek caught Bruin's eye. There was something about the half-caste's manner that made both of them want to smile.

Bruin spoke first and his words cut across any sense of amusement either of them might have had.

"Why did you kill Jansen, Timmers?" he asked.

Timmers wriggled his toes on the board floor, opened his eyes a little wider but still did not raise them. He did not answer.

Van Reebek allowed the silence to go on for a long time. Timmers looked up at him out of the corners of his eyes. Presently Van Reebek asked:

"Is there to be a new song sung in the barrack tonight?"

Still Timmers kept his silence.

"If you do not talk," threatened Van Reebek, "we shall have to put you alone in a dark room until you do."

Timmers' eyebrows drew together. But he still stood wordless.

Suddenly and unexpectedly Van Reebek leaned forward and slapped the little man's face, hard.

Timmers straightened up, wide-eyed, and looked at the Lieutenant in astonishment. Then there were tears in his eyes.

"But I did it for you, Mijnheer," he said.

Van Reebek frowned. Bruin asked:

"Why did you do it for the Lieutenant? Explain."

"It was Jansen who had the Lieutenant beaten. I saw him often talking to the Yaponser sergeant and the others. He told them to beat the Lieutenant. He was a bad man."

"God damn it," said Van Reebek; then to Timmers, "Go and wait outside. I will call you again."

Timmers did not move. "You are angry because I killed the pig?" he asked.

"Go," exploded Van Reedek. "Go and wait outside."

Timmers looked puzzled, but saluted and withdrew.

Van Reebek turned to Bruin. "Well, what do we do?" he asked.

The hint of ironic humour was back in Bruin's eyes.

"Tell him to go away and not kill anyone else," he suggested.

Van Reebek shrugged. "Seriously, it is about all we can do. We cannot give him to the Japanese, or put him in solitary confinement ourselves, because we have to ask their permission to do a thing like that. If we made up some other tale, told the Yaps that he was guilty of some other crime, they might decide to take the punishment into their own hands."

"Quite apart from the fact that the camp will be a better place without Jansen," added the Doctor.

"Then perhaps we had better fête the man, instead of punishing him? No, we must be serious."

Bruin shook his head.

"How can we be serious when there is a death almost every day in the camp? Why should we be concerned because an innocent man—for he is mad and therefore not accountable for his actions—causes another death?"

"But he may get the idea that we approve and go about killing anyone and everyone."

"Yes, especially people who are unpleasant to you. Soon you would have no enemies and your job would be a much easier one."

"Oh, do stop talking nonsense."

"I'm sorry—but it is no more nonsense than suggesting that you punish him. If you are going to make an impression with him you must talk on his level. He is mad, you must be mad too."

Van Reebek looked at his companion with a light in his eyes.

"You are right. Wait now while I think." After a few moments he called for Timmers to come in again.

"Timmers," said Van Reebek, "you are a clever man. You know as few men do that it is easy to kill a man. Is that no so?"

"Ja, Mijnheer, it is easy. It is even possible to do it with a long pin."

"Perhaps," said Van Reebek, "it is more difficult *not* to kill men?"

Timmers considered this.

"When they are bad men," he replied, after a pause, "it is indeed difficult not to kill them."

"It is then as I thought," said Van Reebek. "Now who, Mijnheer, would you say was the more clever man, one who does something difficult or one who does something easy?"

"The one who does the difficult things."

"Good. You will then be a clever man. And when you find it difficult not to kill somebody—you will think of this—and you will remember to do the difficult thing—and not kill him."

Timmers narrowed his eyes.

"You are trying to be clever now, Lieutenant," he said. "You are trying to stop me from killing bad people, people who deserve to be killed."

Van Reebek was nonplussed.

Bruin said quietly:

"Look, Timmers, the Lieutenant is not trying to be clever, he is trying to save you trouble. If the Japanese find out that you are killing people, then they will probably kill you, not quickly like you kill, but slowly and with much pain. He is trying to save you now as he saved you at the guard-house."

Timmers thought that over.

"It is true. Of course it is true," he said, and then a look of anxiety came in his eyes. "But the Yaponser don't know anything about Jansen, do they? Nobody had told them? They were saying in the barrack that you said it was a failure of the heart, Doctor."

"And what did you say in the barrack?"

"Nothing. Doctor."

"Then continue to say nothing. The Japanese have ears in every place in the camp." It was Van Reebek who spoke.

Timmers stood still looking from one to the other. Then tears started running down his cheeks again.

"You are good to me, Lieutenant," he said. "I am a silly old man, weak and not very clever at all, save at killing, that is. You are good too, Doctor." Another pause. "May I go now?"

"Yes," said Van Reebek slowly. "Go—but kill no more men, for I will not have you killing, for my sake or for any other reason. Also for your sake. This evening you will bring me all your knives so that you shall not have them by you to tempt you to kill—but will have to come to me for one when you need it and we can then discuss the matter before you go off on your own. It is understood?"

"Ja, Mijnheer."

"Good."

3

When Timmers was out of earshot Van Reebek sighed and leaned back against the board wall behind his head.

Bruin collected the soiled dressings into a kidney bowl and took them outside. As soon as he came back, Van Reebek said:

"We have another problem—who is to succeed Jansen at the cookhouse?"

Bruin nodded. "Yes—that, too, is a problem. Have you any ideas?"

"Not one. Have you?"

Bruin sat down, took his glasses off and lay back on his bed-space. Without his glasses his blue eyes lost some of their awareness and his myopia made him look sleepy and withdrawn. He was, in fact, tired, and yawned.

"Well," he said, "you might find Burns quite good in the job."

Van Reebek flushed.

"I do not think he and I would get on very well. He speaks loudly about people like myself, about" Van Reebek took a breath—"half-castes."

Bruin turned over so that he faced his companion.

"It did not seem to me when I was talking to him this morning that he had a bad opinion of you. He was asking after your health and regretting that you should have had this trouble on your first day as Camp Commandant."

"How did he know that? How did he know that I was to be Commandant?"

"I asked him that. He said the old man had told him."

Van Reebek frowned. "I do not understand. Why should the Commandant have told him, when he has told no one else?"

"I do not know. Perhaps we had better go and ask him. Do you think you can walk over to that barrack all right?"

"Oh yes, there is nothing wrong with me now except that I feel I must have fought fifteen rounds with a world heavy-weight champion."

Van Reebek was not very steady on his feet when he stood up. Pulses beat in every bruise and wound on his face. He was glad of Bruin's arm to begin with, though he dropped it as soon as they were outside. He made a good show of sauntering with his natural stride, but it cost him an effort. He felt many eyes were turned on him, and with a comforting glow he realised that in most of them there was admiration.

The Poisoned Frog's attack on him had been very opportune and might help considerably when it came to be general knowledge that he was going to take over the camp from the Commandant.

In the hospital barrack they found the old man had just had his bath and it had woken him for a while out of his apathy.

He grunted with amusement when he saw Van Reebek's face and said:

"Are you going to bring a case against the Poisoned Frog, for assault and battery?"

Van Reebek had expected sympathy and perhaps a pat on the back; he felt nettled and made no answer.

Bruin said, "He has had a lively day to start his job." And he told the Commandant about Jansen's death. The Commandant listened with his dead stare on Bruin's lips. Occasionally he allowed his bubble-level eyes to slide over Van Reebek. At the end he said:

"Well, I expect the camp will feel relieved about that. Who are you going to pick to take Jansen's place?" His breath was coming very irregularly and only, it seemed, on occasions when he thought about it.

Van Reebek said: "Naturally I had never thought about it before. The Doctor suggests Burns."

The Commandant looked at Bruin. "No wonder we always got on so well together, Jan. One thought always served us both. Yes, I too would suggest Burns. I think he is incorruptible. He will be on his mettle too."

"Huth, why did you tell him that Van Reebek was going to take over from you? You told no one else, did you?"

The Commandant shut his eyes—the lids closing down like a drop curtain behind a wide proscenium arch.

Bruin and Van Reebek stood waiting for his reply, but when he spoke again it was of something else.

"We shall have to make your appointment official, Van Reebek," he said. "Jan, bring the Doctors and the officers in, will you? The sooner we get it done, the sooner I can rest. So long as I am in charge, people can still come and ask me silly questions, like the one you have just asked me, and that vexes me."

Bruin laughed. "You do not still have to keep Van Reebek and me in our places. We both know that you are the boss, even if he is going to take over."

The Commandant opened his eyes again and looked steadily at Bruin, and the Doctor read in his eyes the old man's knowledge that he would die soon, and he wondered uneasily if somehow he had not found out about the B1. The Commandant took a deep breath that might have been a sigh and said:

"I have never had to keep you in your place, Jan: you knew it too well. You were always in the right spot, wherever and whenever I needed you. And Van Reebek too, though I do not suppose he ever realised it, has been the perfect subordinate. Now get the others."

Half an hour later all save the officer who was out with the working-party were gathered at the foot of the Commandant's bed-space or were sitting at the foot of the neighbouring patients' bed-spaces. Bruin stood by to translate, for there were several who spoke little or no English.

The Commandant was propped up in a sitting position, and in his rubbery, expressionless features his eyes were as alive as they had ever been, though to be so wide awake was obviously costing him a great effort.

"First, gentlemen," he said, "let me wish you a Merry Christmas and express the hope, that we must all undoubtedly share, that by the next Feast of Saint Nicholas we shall be free men again." At this, and led by one who was more sentimental than the others, the whole party in turn came forward and shook hands with the old man and they all expressed in one way or another their wishes that he should soon be about the camp again.

Afterwards, the Commandant took another deep breath and went on:

"And now I have some other news for you. My doctors have advised me that if I am to recover I must be freed for a while of the responsibility of the command here. That is true, Doctor DeGoyer, is it not?" Doctor Bruin was surprised to hear an edge of malice in the old man's voice and wondered why it should be there on this occasion.

"Exactly, Mijnheer Commandant," replied DeGoyer suavely, bowing.

"In my place, to act as my deputy and to take over complete command, I am appointing Lieutenant Van Reebek." In the pause that he made there was complete silence. "He is young, strong and courageous and with a high sense of duty. I am confident that he will serve the best interests of all the camp with the utmost of his ability." He paused again, then concluded, "That is all, except that I trust that you will serve him as well as you have served me."

The group of officers, no longer as enthusiastic as they had been, saluted and moved off, breaking up into small groups to discuss what they had heard, some incredulously, some with an acceptance which grew as they thought about it, all with surprise.

Bruin was just settling the Commandant back on his mat when DeGoyer and Den Hertog returned. They were both agitated.

DeGoyer, however, had control of himself.

"May I speak with you a minute, Kapitan?" he asked.

The Commandant yawned. "If you must," he said.

"I think you have probably overlooked the fact that Den Hertog here is the senior military officer in the camp. And it should naturally follow that he should take over command."

"I have not overlooked it. Captain Den Hertog is, as I know well, actually considered senior to me. He never, however, offered to come forward and take any responsibility from me when I was in need of help. He has always preferred to sit back and let others, even his sergeant, do his work for him. So it never entered my mind that he would like to take over now."

"But he is willing, Kapitan."

"And too late. He and you, my good friend, have as we say in my country—missed the 'bus. Have you anything else concerning the camp command that you wish to discuss? If you have, I suggest that you talk it over between you and see Van Reebek with it."

DeGoyer chewed his under lip.

"There will be more heard about this," he said.

But the Commandant was not listening. He was looking in his rucksack, and he paused once or twice as if in surprise. Once he almost spoke, then decided against it and went back to his rummaging.

When at last he looked up, he held a twisted and battered Kooa cigarette, and DeGoyer and Den Hertog were gone.

The Commandant turned a speculative look on to Bruin, who still stood there, a look which puzzled the Doctor, because he saw in the Commandant's eyes a look of puzzlement too.

The Doctor went down the barrack and got a cigarette from a man who was smoking and brought it back to give the Commandant a light from it.

Then he asked, "Are you all right, Huth?"

"Yes, Jan, thank you. Yes, er—no, never mind. Go now and come back later; I want to talk to you about DeGoyer."

Bruin went down the barrack to return the cigarette he had borrowed and for the first time that day he did not feel sure of himself. Something was bothering the Commandant —something other than Den Hertog's desire to take the place of Van Reebek—and the Doctor could not think what it was.

CHAPTER III

The evening air bore the sound of singing. From one part of the camp came the music of a guitar and the astringent music of a song from Amboina. It was a song in which an element of the romantic music which the Spaniards had brought to the East Indies combined with a lingering background that never seemed to catch up with the melody and which had its origin in Hindu temple music.

From the hospital barrack came the sound of Christian carols.

In both places the songs were being sung by groups who favoured harmony and sang clearly, with the ear for music that is common to Dutch and Indonesians.

The carols were being sung with more melancholy and nostalgia than the East Indian songs. The still fresh-looking young Indonesians sang with enjoyment, because their spirits were high and because they enjoyed making music.

The Europeans sang with their minds full of nostalgia, full of memories of small, neat, brick houses in a flat, snowy landscape. Some of them remembered having sung these same carols crunching in the snow and standing to sing in the warm yellow light that beamed into the streets from windows decorated with Christmas trees and shining, multi-coloured glass balls.

Now they stood, gaunt, spectral and dimly lit, in the middle of the hospital barrack and sang with the sound of yearning and misery in their voices. They had been forgotten by the outside world, but they had not forgotten.

Everywhere in the barrack men lay and listened to them, and the voices of the singers expressed the ache that was so strong in nearly all of them. Many men in the barrack knew they would die without ever seeing the red brick houses again, and the pain was sweet while it was almost unendurable.

One man, however, was not caught in the net of painful

homesickness with all the others. He was still scraping his aluminium dixie with his spoon, fearful of leaving even a trace of the pig-fat to be washed off and lost. The grating of his spoon strained the sensibilities of those around him and made them curse him out loud. An orderly went over and took the man's dish from him. As it was taken away the sick man burst into tears.

Outside, in the dark, in the open spaces between the huts, Sergeant Yoshimitsu prowled like a countryman alone for the first time in a big city. A number of things made him restless. The night air carried musky scents across the water from the mainland, the prisoners' singing was unsettling, he had again ordered the guards to keep away from the prisoners and was uneasy lest the men in his charge should take advantage of the opportunity to brew mischief when they were not being closely watched. The failing of the Commandant also caused him anxiety. In his own way he regarded the old man as a friend, as the man among two thousand aliens on whom he could depend to behave in a manner comprehensible to a Japanese.

Yoshimitsu's prowling brought him to the door of the sick barrack that was beside the Commandant's bed-space. The Sergeant had moved silently and no one noticed him standing in the dim light just outside the door frame. From where he stood Yoshimitsu could see the old man as he lay with his eyes shut, could see the irregular and laboured rise and fall of his chest.

In profile to the Sergeant, with his back to the wall and sitting by the Commandant's feet, was Doctor Bruin. He had his hand on the Commandant's ankle and was looking at the carollers with the corners of his mouth drawn down in a grimace that might have denoted physical pain.

Yoshimitsu stood silently for several minutes, until a prisoner surprised him by coming up behind him and halting in the doorway and calling loudly "Kyotski".

The singing stopped and all who could turned and bowed to the shadowy figure in the doorway. Yoshimitsu wanted to curse the man who had called for the usual salutation, but instead he took a short pace forward, returned the salute with extra punctilio, then turned on his heel and left the barrack with quick, businesslike strides.

Bruin, who had been roused from thoughts that were dim

with an uncomfortable misery, watched the light-stepping figure moving away into the darkness and was not sure whether he wanted to spit or run after the man and put his hand on his shoulder.

The choir resumed their singing. They sang "Stille Nacht".

The Commandant opened his eyes and beckoned to Bruin to bend close so that he could whisper to him.

"Do not let them go on, Jan," he said. "This is enough. They will kill some of the men in here if they make them suffer any more."

Bruin shook his head.

"I do not agree," he said. "This is a sort of catharsis—if they cry they will feel better."

The Commandant shook his head. "They are too near the bottom of the well to cry, Jan. Only clear, fresh tears cleanse. The sludge at the bottom is like bile."

Bruin nodded. "You are probably right," he said. Getting up, he went and spoke to the leader of the choir.

As he approached he noticed Smith among those who had been singing. He looked like a man who was dream-walking.

After Bruin had told the leader to stop the singing, and on behalf of the sick men had thanked the choir, he went and spoke to the priest.

"Are you all right, Padre?" he asked.

Smith looked at him as if he did not recognise him.

"Yes," he said. "Yes, I am all right, thank you."

He followed the others out and on to the next barrack.

After the choir had left, DeGoyer and Schiller came up the barrack together and stopped by Wim Peterson's bed-space on the shelf. The Doctor carried a hypodermic syringe.

Peterson did not realise what was happening. He felt the sudden prick of the needle and saw DeGoyer's wide mouth twisted in a grin.

"We are going to make you better, boy," the Doctor said, as he slowly eased the plunger of the syringe down. "Right from this minute, now, you will begin to feel something has happened to you that is a good thing."

Peterson rolled his head on his head-rest. "No," he said, "I am not going to get better."

DeGoyer asked, "Will you take a bet with me? By tomorrow morning you will be feeling a little better. This is

140

a Christmas Day you will remember all your life. What will you bet me?"

But Wim only shook his head.

The Doctor shrugged, withdrew the needle, wiped the tiny wound and said:

"You are inclined to be ungrateful; tomorrow you will feel differently." He moved off. Schiller pulled the sarong down around the boy's legs again and patted his hand.

"The Doctor speaks the truth," he said. "God has been merciful to you."

"Be better tomorrow." The words repeated in Wim Peterson's mind. It was a joke. It could not be. Tomorrow was too soon.

Further down the barrack, Bruin, watching the Commandant, thought tomorrow was doubtful. Tomorrow might be the end.

2

In Den Hertog's barrack the Indonesians still sang their native songs. The barrack had a festive atmosphere that existed in the other Indonesian barracks as well.

In the European barracks there was an atmosphere of mourning: every man in them was alive only when he thought of the past, for there was almost no foreseeable future.

The Indonesians lived in the present and found it not so terrible, not so sharply different from their normal existences before they had been made prisoners. Much that was around them had been familiar since childhood. A mat to sleep on after a long day of coolie labour in the hot sun, a diet of rice with, this evening, a flavour of pork, and now the liberty to sing. They were at home and did not have to dream backwards to a different key of existence in a different colour range. The hot nights, the heavy green of the vegetation, sweat, the exuberance of both animal and plant growth—all these were as common to them as smoky chimneys were to the Europeans.

What they lacked was the presence of their neatly made women with their subdued voices and sparkles of laughter. These they lacked, so they sang of them. Quite often their songs were sentimental, but leavened now and then with a sort of intimate humour that would have seemed shocking to the minds of white men brought up, unnaturally, to regard the function of creative talent that is common to all life as something obscene and degrading.

To these boys and men the act of copulation was a joyous thing and, though it was carried out in some degree of privacy, its joys, as were all joys, were made to be shared.

Christ was, to many of them, only a name given to a day of holiday, and as a holiday they celebrated it.

At one end of the barrack two white men were practising the Christian principle for this day.

DeGoyer was saying slowly:

"Let us not waste time pretending that we are shocked. The thing is that the man has been put in over your head and has thus deprived you and me too, as your friend, of an opportunity to improve our positions in the camp. So we must find some way to discredit him with the others. Then, when the old man is gone, we can shift Van Reebek by weight of popular opinion."

Den Hertog shook his head. "And then get myself chosen in his place by weight of popular opinion? It would not work. I am not a popular man. We would unseat Ven Reebek only to find someone else in his place. No, what we have to do is to make Van Reebek serve our ends."

"How?" DeGoyer asked. "The Englishman picked Van Reebek knowing how difficult it would be for anyone to do that."

Den Hertog nodded. "True—but you forget he is also a regular army officer, and I am very much his senior."

DeGoyer laughed. "Do you think he is going to obey you, then?"

"Do you think I am a fool? Listen." Den Hertog leaned forward. "Who is the principal enemy of our country? Germany, isn't it? Before the Japs came in Van Reebek was one of the leading younger officers in the 'N.S.B.' He did a special course of training in Germany. After the war he will want to keep all that very quiet, for after the war our people will be as anti-German as they were pro-German before it started."

"So?"

"So we threaten him with exposure—I shall say that I will bring him to court martial as a traitor. You will see then what kind of a tune he will sing. He is a professional, but his profession will be gone and so will his reputation. They might even imprison him."

"We can try it," said DeGoyer uncertainly. "We can try it. Now?"

"Yes, now, while he is unsettled and nervous about taking over. He will want to have as few people working against him as possible. We will tell him that we shall be discreet. He will perhaps try to have us on his side to begin with—and then once we are in . . ." Den Hertog shrugged.

DeGoyer was still unconvinced. He knew Den Hertog to be instinctively the cloak-and-dagger type of conspirator, seldom in touch with reality: and he, DeGoyer had made himself the man he was by his ability to judge human character. Van Reebek he knew was not a man to be frightened easily. He must be removed. But then, the Doctor thought, and as Den Hertog had said, someone even less friendly to the Doctor's interests might be put in. But again, anyone, any officer in the camp would be more likely than Van Reebek to play the kind of game DeGoyer required. So if they got him out it could only be to the good. Suddenly it occurred to DeGoyer that Den Hertog knew this and was afraid that he, DeGoyer, would double-cross him, would desert him for any new Commandant. He was right. Of course he would. Well, all that would be seen later. They might as well try Den Hertog's plan. They would not lose by it, and they just might strike lucky when, as Den Hertog had said, the young man was newly appointed and nervous.

When they got to the Doctor's billet, where Van Reebek was now settled, they found him in the small, cell-like room alone. Bruin was still with the Commandant and Smith was sitting out on the verandah staring blankly into the darkness towards the sea.

Van Reebek was lying down resting his sore and aching head.

He sat up when the two men came in. For the second time that day he felt himself cornered by enemies. He was surprised to find himself quite without anxiety, only full of anger.

"Well, Mijnherren?" he said a they entered.

"We came to see how you were, my dear Van Reebek," said DeGoyer. "Are the wounds better?"

"Doctor Bruin is treating them, thank you, Doctor."

"So? You sound in a bad humour. It is natural after such a trying day. I trust you will not find your new position too—too—shall I say—exacting."

"That depends on the way the officers and the men in the camp behave."

Den Hertog said, "You take a very superior attitude, Jonje, with your 'officers and men in the camp'."

Van Reebek said nothing.

"Well, we have come to offer you our help, as you are after all young and inexperienced."

"Thank you," said Van Reebek. "I am sure it will be very useful."

"Ah, I am glad you are going to be reasonable."

"I shall try to be reasonable as long as you are."

DeGoyer shook his head; this was not getting them anywhere.

"I was interested to hear from Den Hertog that you were a member of the National Socialistiche Beweging at home."

Van Reebek actually smiled. Now he knew what to expect.

"A lot of young men in the army were members of it, Doctor. The Germans know the way to provide inspiring military leadership: it was something manifestly lacking among the older men in our army."

DeGoyer laughed and turned to Den Hertog. "He means people like you, my friend," he said.

Den Hertog flushed. "Those who were members of the 'N.S.B.' will not be allowed to be insubordinate after the war."

Van Reebek shrugged. "When the war is over will be time enough to talk about that. But perhaps it will be well for you to remember, Captain, that our army in Java did not make a very good showing against the Japanese. Perhaps some of the senior officers of that time may find some difficulties in their way after the war as well."

DeGoyer got up, leaned against the wall and looked down speculatively at the Lieutenant. The young man was no fool, he thought; in fact he would follow well in the tradition of the old English Commandant. One would respect him as an enemy and perhaps try to make a friend of him. He would need friends, for most of the men, particularly the white men, he was going to have to command were many years older than he was.

144

Schiller was in desperation.

He would not give up. There must be an answer. It was a long time before it began to dawn on him that he was not really just asking for an answer—but was asking for the only answer he wanted to hear.

He had been praying for nearly three hours when this fact became clear to him, and he lay down and closed his eyes to try to think out how he should act now that he knew that his desires were, in part at least, selfish.

He wanted the Commandant to live. He believed that he had the power to give him life. But was it only to satisfy his own desires that he asked to be allowed to steal and make this gift?

Schiller turned restlessly on his mat. Once or twice he got up to answer calls from sick men. Once he walked down the barrack again to look at the old man. Then he went back and lay awake, on and on through the night.

CHAPTER IV

DOCTOR Bruin's wife was named Renate and she was by birth a German. To look at, she was dark and boyish. She emphasised this latter trait by wearing her hair in a short crop. In her unconscious libertinism she was as graceful as a wild animal. She had a compulsion to practise sex that was a part of her fundamental nature.

Bruin was possessive. She was his. By marrying her he had saved her from becoming, as she had once put it herself, "a rather superior sort of tart". Bruin adored her so long as she remained truly his.

During their life together, up to the time when they were separated by the war, they had been happy. She had been very content to be his wife. He pleased her in every way: she admired his strength of character, he was a clean-living, vigorous man, a natural leader and a satisfactory lover. He knew he pleased her, and in turn she gave him all he needed, a certain elegance that was natural and not sophisticated, a quiet home life where his will was treated with respect, but not slavishly so. And, although she would have loved to have had a son, she was undoubtedly a good mother to her daughters, one of whom was going to be strikingly beautiful.

As Bruin lay in his billet in the dark and thought of her, the Commandant intruded into his memories. What would the old man have thought of her? Bruin had little more than mentioned her name to him, and even that had been a concession: for he never spoke of her to anyone for fear that, by allowing her to be even ever so lightly touched by others, she might be tarnished by the contact. But now he rather wished that he had talked with the Commandant about her. The old man was by nature careful in the way that he handled things which he knew meant a lot to others: and he had a gift for turning them gently as if they might be precious stones and finding some odd hidden facet that would shine only for him. He was virtually selfless, but, in fact, and in a quiet way, he was always building a little bit more on to himself. He seemed to spend his time thinking of others, and yet behind this screen of abnegation he was every day forging the steel of his own character, refining himself through the deliberate subjection of his interests to those of the people who depended upon him.

What new discovery might he have made in the character of Renate? Bruin wondered. It was probably too late now ever to find out.

Then the Doctor had a sudden revelation. He realised that, in having refused to help the Commandant and give him a chance of survival, he too was showing the kind of unselfishness that was so typical of the old man. For really, he, Bruin, so he thought, was the one person in the camp who was going to feel his friend's death more bitterly than anyone else.

Bruin had often told himself in the past that the Commandant would have had a job to get along without him. For the Commandant was, if anything, too soft, too gentle, though with surprising streaks of intuitive ruthlessness, to command men who had sunk to the low ebb of behaviour common to most of the men in the camp. To the Doctor, the Commandant was not sufficiently a pragmatist to live the kind of life forced on prisoners of war. He had started out with too much idealism, too much faith in human nature. He, Bruin, had been born a cynic, so that the life he lived now had not come as such a surprise to him and he had been able to adapt his manner and outlook quite easily.

Yet, thought Bruin, which of us is going to come out of this bitter trial the best? I with my cynicism more watertight and deeply founded than ever before, or the Commandant with a new faith, a new creed that brings him, and may well bring others, a sense of purpose and completeness?

In the dark, Doctor Bruin shrugged and turned his thoughts back to his wife. He had a game that he used to play. He used to pick out of his memory a day that they had spent together and with great labour build it back, piece by piece, like a jig-saw puzzle, until it was as complete as he could make it.

Sometimes he would recreate the whole of the day in such perfect detail that he almost brought Renate to life and forgot to be jealous of her.

Van Reebek was snoring. His sleep was a profound one, and he was to be grateful for it when he awoke to face another day's anxieties, for it gave him strength to meet them. Earlier, when he lay down, in contrast with Bruin, his relaxation had not been disturbed by jealousy for his wife; in fact, he was unmarried. Nor had he Smith's metaphysical qualms of conscience. He was healthily tired and rather pleased with himself. He had fought a good fight during the day, and gained confidence as a result of it. He thought of himself no longer as a half-caste. He was a man amongst men who were all the same, save that he, out of nearly two thousand, was the one who had been picked to be the leader. Though he knew the future was not going to be easy, he knew too that he would be able to face it and win through, or at least show that he had enough mettle to go down fighting.

He lay between Bruin and Smith, and his snores disturbed the latter as the sound of children laughing might disturb a man waiting to be led to the gibbet to be hung. It was such a natural, healthy sound.

Smith had reached a crisis. Like Schiller in another hut, he could make no contact with God. Unlike Schiller, however, who believed that the Divinity was merely withholding his Grace, Smith had come to the house and found it empty. He had believed in the possibility of salvation, but the Hand that should have rescued him was an empty promise and was not there, had never been there. He was afloat in a sea, in the night. He found himself surprisingly buoyant, yet full of terror: for he knew he was drifting towards some form of disaster. It was a slow, agonising drift made in a delirium.

"Give it reality." He was not sure when those words had first come to his mind, but they were insistent now, timing themselves to fall between Van Reebek's snores. Snore—"give it reality"—snore—"give it reality." But what? Give what reality? The drift—the sea? Escape that way? Why not? The end must come soon. Perhaps if a guard saw him he would shoot. Then it would be a very swift way. Of course the guard would shoot. He would think it was a man trying to escape. Little yellow monkey, he would be right. It would not be suicide either: he would have to lie alone in unconsecrated ground.

Smith sat up.

The others would think he was going to the latrine, that is if either of them heard him.

As he moved slowly down his bed-space to the alleyway at the end of it, Smith became aware for the first time in his life of the details of existence. He saw everything about him neatly and clearly. As if for the only time, he saw them in sharp focus. Everything made patterns and shapes and had clean, sharp edges, even in the semi-darkness. He saw his own bare feet hunting for the leather instep strap of his wooden sandals. He saw and felt beneath his hand the edge of the bedding-board, and its clean right angles and solidity had a calming effect on him. To be able to hold it firmly steadied his resolve. The room was like a small, dark box, the two little windows stamped out of the two walls squarely and barred against the faint light of a waning moon. Some of the loom of the moonlight fell on Van Reebek's sleeping face, making the skin blue and throwing shadows under the swelling bruises that stood up from his cheekbones and along the line of the right side of his jaw.

Smith moved as quietly as he could towards the door. He was not interested in animate things any more. Bruin and Van Reebek, so still in their sleep, meant less to him than the twisted perspectives of the verandah outside, which was revealed in the pale light through the building's front door.

Outside, the beaten earth path that led to the billet was oddly luminous and the leaves of the gardenia bushes were black. The flowers on them were a dead white, and their scent mingling with the scent from the jasmine creepers was fumey and sickly.

Smith moved openly and determinedly over the hundred yards that separated the hut from the bathing-beach. The sentry-post was another hundred yards on, so there was no fear of the guard seeing him and rushing him before he could get into the water.

A few little puffs of wind came to Smith across the sand, and although it was warm and humid, he felt his skin rise in goose-flesh.

The moon went behind a cloud, and immediately afterwards the sentry called something and clicked the bolt of his rifle.

From where the Korean stood the figure on the edge of the sea was very ill-defined. The man screwed his eyes up trying to make sure whether he had really seen a man moving across the beach or whether in his drowsy state he had only imagined it.

Smith waded out into the sea. The water, like the air, was warm. At any moment he expected to hear a rifle shot; then he laughed at himself, thinking that if the aim was good he would not hear the shot.

The Korean, holding his rifle across his body, came down from his post towards the beach. He was just going to raise his gun to his shoulder to fire at the white blob he could see against the darker background of the sea when it started to rain.

First one or two big, heavy drops, then a quick patter and finally, like the descent of a vast squared block of basalt, the torrent fell, obliterating everything. The Korean ran hastily back to the protection of his hut and stood wondering what he should do. Reason told him that the man he had seen enter the water could not be trying to escape. There was no escape on that side of the island, where the tide ran strongly and a man would have to swim miles before he came to another shore. Then why had the man entered the sea? Perhaps to get cool. But what man would risk getting shot for the sake of getting cool? The Korean was a man of severely limited intelligence and no imagination: when a problem became too great for the scope of his mind he set it aside, with the intention of coming back to it again later, and the certain knowledge that he would never come back to it.

If one of the prisoners was missing when the count was made in the morning no one would be able to blame him, for no one would know what had become of the man.

Meanwhile, Smith had gone on walking out to sea until he was beyond his depth. Then he stared to swim, still moving away from the shore. He had just got out of the inshore eddies and into the main run of the ride when the storm broke.

For a moment he could not think what had happened. He had not noticed the first drops, and the full weight of the rain therefore broke on him without warning.

He at once became confused. The rain struck the sea like millions of little projectiles and raised a fine mist of spray to the height of nearly a foot. It also struck phosphorescent sparks off the surface. Smith was soon fighting for breath, for the air was saturated with spray. The phosphorescence alarmed him. At the level of his eyes he seemed to be already submerged, shallowly, just below the surface of a sea that was burning upwards with jets of fire which rose like flames from a gas-ring.

He panicked. There was no deliberation now in his movements, only the urgency to breathe, to somehow get air into his lungs and to keep his air passages clear of water.

He had no sense of direction left and struck out wildly, swimming in erratic sweeps this way and that. It was not long before he exhausted himself, and he was surprised at one moment to hear someone calling for help.

After a long while there was a searing pain in his knee and, almost before he had been able to register it, a tremendous impact on his left shoulder. He thrashed the water again wildly and the pain was in his right heel. Then one of his flailing arms struck something rough and hard, something that did not move when he brought the flat of his hand down on it.

For a moment he could not believe his senses; then he realised he was in shallow water and among rocks.

He had arrived without knowing it at the extremity of the island where a rocky spit stuck out into the tideway. He was caught now and held by the eddy which developed inwards along the shore. He bumped other parts of his body severely, several times, before at last he succeeded in crawling out of the water on to a piece of smooth rock.

Presently a part of his mind started to work again and he sat up. The rain had stopped, but in the thick undergrowth, which started only a few feet from his head, the water dripped and trickled and filled the night with as much noise as a shallow river might make running over a bed of many stones. There were gusts, too, of a hot smell of decaying vegetation that came off the earth behind him like stale body-odour.

Smith sank his head on his hands and sat in that attitude trying to focus his mind on his dilemma, trying to make sense of his present situation.

The moon came out from behind the clouds. Smith was not aware of its light until he raised his head. Then he saw to his right, less than half a mile away, the sandy beach down which he had walked into the sea. It seemed very clear. Someone, probably a sentry, lit a match and the pin-point of light against the darkness of the trees was as though someone had struck a pinhole in a black silhouette and held it to the light.

Over there, Smith thought, men were alive and sleeping. By now, for all they knew, he might have been dead.

What should he do? Go on and carry out his original intention?

He was at once filled again with the blind terror he had just suffered in the sea.

It was a long time before he realised that it was either that or try to get back into the camp.

This thought frightened him too.

He would have to get back undetected; otherwise, if he were caught by the guards—he remembered Van Reebek's mutilated face as he had seen it in the moonlight when he had left his hut.

There was no thought of prayer in Smith's mind. He had accepted the fact that he had been deserted so completely that he would not turn to God now. He would have liked to stay where he was, unmoving and without having to make any decision. He felt utterly unattached and in a void. There seemed to be no reason why he should move, why he should do anything.

He put his hands on the rock behind him and let his head fall back. Above him the moon was nearing a cloud, illuminating one edge of it so that it shone like untidy silver hair fringing out from beneath a black skullcap.

He was watching the moon and the movements of the clouds with a faintly dizzy feeling, because they were reeling over his head so quickly, when he heard a sound that might have been made by a piece of rouch wood being dragged across the rocks. And then, before he had even time to turn, bony, cold fingertips were creeping across his right hand as it lay outstretched on the rock. Smith froze and almost fainted, to be brought back to life by an agonising, searing pain in one finger. He drew both his hands together and leaped to his feet. Something lifted with his hand, then fell away, and as he turned he saw the thing. In the dim light it looked like a cudgel, black and square-headed. It scuttled across the rock and disappeared in a fissure.

Smith examined his injured finger and found the flesh broken and bleeding. But now he had recovered his senses. He sucked the finger and looked about for other helmet crabs, for it was one of these creatures which, he realised, must have bitten him.

Then he raised his head and looked up to the sky again.

He saw the brilliant glow of the moon, reappearing this time from a cloud, reappearing like a dazzling presence.

Smith was not a man to avoid the obvious imagery. He was looking to the sky, to heaven. He did not see the infinity of space there; the darkness was not penetrable, it was a ceiling studded with stars: Smith stood in a sub-basement. Above stairs there was all the golden glory of a palace, a treasure-house, and the radiance there emanated from the simple figures of God the Father, Son and Holy Ghost and all the archangels. For a moment the radiance of one of those countenances had been turned towards him. He had been warned, punished and saved. In the reappearance of the moon he had the sign which said: "Go and sin no more."

He had been forgiven, but somewhere at the back of his mind he knew that his sin went beyond the fact that he had tried to take his own life; it was greater than that. He would pray earnestly for it to be revealed to him. And at the thought he went on his knees and started to pray for guidance. As he knelt he opened his eyes every little while and glanced round to see that the rock remained clear of helmet crabs.

3

Wim Peterson was woken by the sound of rain on the corrugated iron roof. But it was more than that which woke him. It was the intolerable pressure that he felt within him on his bladder. Down in his groin it felt as if a knife was being forced into him. He started the laborious crawl to the foot of the bed-boards and was surprised to find that he was able to move a little more easily. He got into the alleyway between the bedding shelves and walked heavily towards the door.

The pain in his groin made him incline his body forward.

It was impossible to go outside. The rain was falling in a deluge. Wim stood in the doorway and urinated out into the streams of water that were pouring from the corrugated iron eaves. Never could he remember having spent so much time passing water. He stood and it poured from him in an arc and ran away down the little gullies in the mud that took the drainings from the roof.

He seemed to have no desire to finish, but could always bring a little more.

At last he went and lay on his bed-space again. As he walked back he felt a difference in the weight of his body. The tight skin of his legs and ankles no longer seemed to be restraining the pressure of the ballooning flesh beneath it. There were the beginnings of deflation. With it there came a lift in his spirits. There was an unexpected release from the oppression that had for so long saddled his every thought and sense.

He lay back in his bed with a sigh.

Already he could feel faintly the need to urinate again, but as yet without any urgency.

As he lay, he thought for the first time for weeks of the possibility of release from captivity. The news he had heard without interest earlier, that the Americans were advancing steadily towards the Philippines, might lead sooner or later to victory for the Allies. If he could only survive, there was so much that would come afterwards. A reunion with his mother. He was certain she would be alive. Perhaps his father too might still be living.

Then he could go to a technical college in Holland. He could almost feel the smooth running of a lathe between his fingertips as he thought of it. Steel filings, the curved piece of steel that comes away from the metal as a thread is put on it: the burnished steel, spinning as it is touched with carborundum: the beautiful satisfaction of making steel fit steel to within hundredths of a millimetre: the smooth, gentle fitting of it, one perfect face to another.

The rain stopped. Wim Peterson got up again and turned and walked the other way down the barrack to the door beside the Commandant's bed-space. The boy was holding his head high and looking straight ahead of him as he walked past the motionless form of the old man.

He went outside, slopping a little in the mud, and stood in front of a tall, galvanised funnel that had its spout buried deep in the ground. This was a camp urinal. They stood everywhere round the huts like large, shallow wine-glasses.

Again he passed water and was amazed at the almost unending stream that flowed from him. A sentry in a pill-box a little way away struck a match and lit a cigarette. He did not bother to conceal the flame of the match, but kept the cigarette cupped within the palm of his hand as he drew from it.

Wim Peterson, too, when he got back to his billet found a cigarette and lit it, drawing the smoke deeply into his lungs with a sense of excitement and satisfaction.

He could appreciate tobacco after weeks of finding a smoke dull and without pleasure.

Instead of lying down again, he sat on the edge of the bedding-boards swinging his heavy legs. But he could swing them. The knee joint was free, or freer.

Wim looked up and down the barrack to his right and left and found that the rows of sick men did not depress him as they had done. Some of them he thought would get better, not many of them—but a few. A few would wake up one day to feel as he did, to feel something warm flowing back into their veins. They would find the taste of a cigarette sweet again. They might feel the desire to sit in the comparatively cool early hours of the morning and swing their legs and look dispassionately up and down the barrack.

Schiller came by, walking from his end of the hut to the Commandant's. Peterson stopped him.

"I am peeing well," he said, "all the time."

Schiller frowned.

"Oh, you are all right," he replied; "you are not going to die."

"I am going to pee myself back to life again." Peterson found the thought delightful and wanted to laugh.

Schiller left him swinging his legs and grinning.

The orderly went and looked at the Commandant and then went back to his own bed-space, still uncertain, still troubled, still seeking conviction.

PART FOUR

—

December 26th, 1944

CHAPTER I

THE Commandant opened his eyes. He was not sure whether he had been asleep or whether he had been comatose and was reviving.

His mind worked as if it were being short-circuited every few moments. The thoughts it threw up were sporadic and disconnected.

"No, I keep telling you, no," he was saying to part of himself, "you are all right. Nothing is going to happen that will hurt. You are past being hurt. The nerve endings are dead. They can stick pins into you and you do not feel them. You are lucky. I am not so lucky. I have still got my senses—most of the time I have—so do not keep bothering me by asking what we are going to do about it. You have gone on ahead of me. You are dead already."

Somebody passed the foot of the bed-space. The Commandant could not make out who it was, for not only was it dark, but even when he looked right at the hurricane lamp where it hung some ten feet away he saw it in soft focus.

He allowed his eyelids to fall back again, curtaining out the muzzy picture.

He noticed again the sweaty smell of the coverings of the man next to him. "Thank God," he thought, "the clothes underneath my head are clean. I do not have to lie in the stink of my own sweat." He tried to move his right leg to meet the other one, for there was a stiffness in his hip joint, an ache in it. He could feel the weight of the leg—it was very heavy—but he only knew that he had raised it and put it down again because of the weight on his thigh muscles which came and went. There was no feeling in his heel or calf.

"Wet beriberi," he said to himself, "is painless. I am lucky not to have dry beriberi, for then my hands and feet would ache. But if they ached, at least I would know I had them."

His mind cut out for a moment, then picked up again.

"Pantiles—red pantiles—and the dark ugliness of a monkey-puzzle tree spreading up in front of them. The tree and its hundreds and thousands of miniature Japanese, no, Chinese, pagodas, are black: a Chinese painting against the evenly wind-rifled tiles."

Nothing.

"I'm not really old. Everyone calls me the 'old man' because they are so young. I am not young, but under normal circumstances I might have fifteen or twenty years to live. For the old, the really aged who dissolve into dust and blow away, death may be easy."

The Commandant heaved his chest round a little, like a man turning a heavy tun. "Two hundred and fifty gallons of wine equals one tun. A tun has iron hoops round it and is heavy like this and awkward.

"The sun-ripe streets of Oporto and that man who had a vineyard and took me to a press. The black, liquid gold that was the old port wine, heavy and rich, crusted and rimed with richness. It hung on the tongue like the taste of pine-filled mountain air.

"I have lived. I have tasted the pines and the wines. What do women taste like? A Chinese, sweet-sour sauce and the fruit of the durian.

"It was raining. It *is* raining."

Schiller stood looking down at the old man. The Commandant did not know he was there. The orderly put his hand into the rucksack, took out the vial of $B1$ and carried it back down the hut with him.

"If only I could breathe without moving my chest. Very small breaths.

"The night is dark; perhaps there is going to be a storm. I am not delirious? No. No fever. Thinking disconnected thoughts.

"It is not a storm. It is a blanket, a thick grey service-blanket. Not that either; it is too big. If you got under it, right in the middle, you might not be able to get out again. Like the man who got under his sail when his boat capsized, racing. The little knob pressing up in the middle of it, like a ripening boil, but pressing up and down. Little thumbhead in a panic trying to push the sail up instead of swimming out from underneath it.

"Perhaps all deaths are like drowning.

"Is death whatever we fear most?

"Death is a grey blanket.

"Or is it lonely? It is so lonely, going out alone!

"The crowd has stopped roaring. There is only the drip of water from the eaves.

"Scrum half is a good place to play, constructive and always in the picture. A ball pointed downwards. The flick of wrists that moves it to Mathews. We work well together. Mathews at stand off is clever with a drop kick. Get a scrum near goal, heeled cleanly, a pass to Mathews. Four points.

"The oil in the lamp must be giving out. Somebody passing my bed again, too.

"Feet like uncooked dumplings, with five little bulbous teats on them. The flesh is pulled in at the toe-roots like the neck of a balloon—but not so tightly.

"Now I must take this seriously. This is a very serious moment.

"Red laterite, not the rich dark brown soil that raises sweet grass, but a red soil that grows stuff on it as a cheese grows cheese mould. It is funny that I should find that that matters.

"Alice. What a nice thought. I knew you, Alice, when Rupert Brooke was the rage: 'One day I think I'll feel a cool wind blowing, see a slow light across the Stygian tide . . . and watch you, a broad-browed and smiling dream, pass, light as ever, through the lightless host . . . and turn and toss your brown delightful head, amusedly, among the—something—dead.'

"Will you be there? With that fat slug of a husband of yours?

"I want a cigarette.

"What happens if I stop remembering to breathe?

"I can't stop remembering.

"I wonder if anybody else will die with me? I am sure some of them would like to. They have got so used to leadership, they might feel safer if they went with me.

"What could I tell them to cheer them up, when they do not find any golden staircases? Poor sods.

"I must take this seriously.

"I wonder how Jan feels about it. He must know. Perhaps he did not expect it would be now. I would like to say goodbye to him. He has gone out of his way for me many times. I shall regret that I did not see him.

"That poor Schiller too. I wonder why he was hiding that stuff in my rucksack. Surely he is not trying to keep it for himself in case he gets beriberi? Though he would be entitled to do that. After all, he does make things easier for most of these poor beggars here: he has a right to keep himself on his feet to serve them. I think he will be sorry to see me go too. I wonder how many others will? I know they like me—nearly all of them—they have told me so in a dozen different ways. That Christmas tree they made for me last year and the little book. How did they manage here, where there is nothing, to make a Christmas tree and a little book full of pictures and appreciation? That must have been a labour of love—and to keep it secret and spring it on me! And when they saw I was pleased and clapped my hands, they all laughed. Hundreds of them. I think that was the peak of my achievement in life.

"And Jan. I *would* like to say goodbye to him. Through him I could say it to all of them. I wonder if I could call Schiller?"

The Commandant opened his eyes. He saw the lamplight dimly for a moment and then it guttered and was gone.

2

Wherever the rain-forest is untouched by man, it is often characterless. All the trees and bushes stand so close together that nothing has identity. It is a matted mass, woven together by great creepers that climb and fall from the trees like the snarl of ship's rigging on the masts of old wooden walls that have grappled in combat and tangled their shrouds and yards one with the other.

Even in daylight the pools of water that stand everywhere are black and filled with a slithering, furtive life.

At night the emphasis is shifted from the density of the mass to the immediate impenetrability of the suffocating wall of greenery that is like the embrace of a fat, unwanted and persistent woman.

Smith had nothing with which to hack his way through the jungle. He had to tear a passage with his hands.

Within a few moments of entering it he was again running

with water, part of it sweat and the rest falling on him from thick green leaves that cupped the water and then spilt it with deliberation.

He could not make his way along the beach because he had immediately come upon a cliff and had had to break inland.

He had to make his way through over a quarter of a mile of the jungle before he came to the clearing on his side of the wire that marked the boundary of the camp. Also he had to try to move without making a noise.

Soon he found he made the most progress by lying flat and forcing himself along on his belly. He had to climb a steep little hummocky hillside. He kept the faint gleam of the water on his left. The earth was tepid underneath him and in many places oozing with soft mud. Roots, unseen at the passage of his head and shoulders, struck him angrily in the ribs. An insect bit him on the soft flesh of his stomach. It was like being struck with a thick, red-hot needle. He had lost his sarong in the sea and was naked. The mud coated his chest and trunk and lay against his pelvis in a wave like a soft cushion. The lower branches of bushes scraped along his back, tearing the skin. Once or twice, reaching out, he grasped a shape that was slimy and slithery. Each time he suffered a shock, thinking it was something with life in it, only to find that it was a bush with a smooth wet bark that had the texture of skin.

Smith barely thought of his difficulties, however. His one desire was to get back into the camp undetected. This urgency made everything else fade into insignificance. He was struggling with the same intensity as he had struggled when he had been in the sea; but then he had been in a panic, now he was filled with resolve.

He must get back to the camp and apply himself to the task of finding out in what way he could best serve his God, for he knew now that he had never served Him, but had always been serving himself. He had worked in the ministry for years, obeyed the rules, observed all that he had been taught, and had done it mechanically, always without spending any part of himself, except it were on himself. He had prayed diligently and sincerely for his own soul's salvation, because that had seemed to be the most important thing he could do: to save himself from the expectancy of hell-fire.

He had proclaimed God's might to those who would listen to him, believing in it utterly and seeing himself all the time as one of the Elect, chosen and therefore blessed with a Divine Right in all he did: a right which protected him from suffering, as an antiseptic may protect a doctor from the diseases of his patients. And because he had been so well protected, he realised, he had never suffered.

He had preached Christ's agony on the Cross and considered his job done. He himself, he believed, had been absolved of all suffering by that great act. He had never considered it something which he ought to share, both with Christ and with others.

As he crawled now on his belly, while he was full of determination to survive and to serve God, he was also full of humility. Though he was desperate, he was sustained by the soft flood of this new feeling which grew in him with every moment until he felt exultant and able to overcome any obstacle that might stand between him and his new conception of duty.

He saw now that if he were ever to be worthy of the great ideal that had been set him by his Leader, he must share the pains of others; that simply to hold aloof from them and offer the words of the Scriptures as consolation was like telling a man who carries a heavy load. "It is not heavy really—you only think it is." From now on he must persuade the man to let him share the load.

Smith reached the edge of the clearing and lay behind a bush watching the line of the fence for the movements of the sentries.

Had he been able to see himself he would never have recognised the blood-smeared, mud-coated, gaunt man as anyone he knew. He might also have been perplexed by the new virility that filled that stranger.

He had nearly two hundred yards of the clearing to cover before he reached the barbed wire. The fence was no more than a demarcation line. It had not been set up with the idea of making it impassable. It stood eight or nine feet high, but the strands of wire were wide apart and not threaded into squares.

To his right, Smith saw the first faint paling of dawn in the sky. The sentry to his left, in the pill-box nearest him, leaned his rifle against the side of his shelter and walked across the two or three yards that separated him from a urinal. He had his back to the priest.

Smith ran quickly across the open ground, fell heavily over the stump of a tree, but recovered himself without pausing to realise that he had knocked all the wind out of his body. He dived through beneath the lowest wire on the fence and the ground. Again he tore the flesh on his back, but he was inside the wire before he felt the pain. The Korean was still standing at the urinal. Smith crept on all fours to the shadows beside the nearest hut, then he stood up and walked as unconcernedly as he could back towards his billet.

On the verandah he paused and for the first time glanced at his own naked body.

He tiptoed into his room.

Van Reebek lay on his side. He had stopped snoring. The Doctor's corner of the room was too dark for Smith to be able to see Bruin properly, but he got the feeling that he was awake.

Smith got the piece of calico he used as a towel and wrapped himself in it.

As he passed the foot of the Doctor's bed again, on his way out, he heard a whispered question:

"Where have you been?"

Smith did not know what to answer; then filled with a sudden bravado he replied:

"Looking for God."

Bruin sat up. He stared at the priest in the dim light for a long time. Then he shook his head and without any comment lay down again.

Smith was just about to turn away when Bruin said:

"I have been awake a long time. I thought I heard you go out. It is nearly dawn, isn't it?"

Smith said, "Yes."

"Where are you going now?"

"To sit on the verandah until I can go into the sea and get washed."

"Sins or mud?"

For a moment Smith felt anger rising in him. Bruin's agnosticism always manifested itself in that kind of humour.

Then he shrugged: he had more important things to be concerned about.

"Quite a lot of both," he replied quietly; and for the first

164

time in his life he found that he had been able to overcome the indignation that had been spontaneous before when someone had made a bantering remark about his beliefs.

Bruin too was surprised. He knew Smith rose habitually to the kind of remark he had just made. He sat up again; then he got up and accompanied the priest on to the verandah, where the light was growing fast. There he saw him properly for the first time.

"Why, damn, man, you are in a mess! There is hardly a square inch of your body that is not scratched or torn."

Smith nodded.

"Yes," he said. "I have learned a lot."

Bruin frowned.

"I do not understand."

Smith did not explain.

3

Schiller's trouble with his religious beliefs had not been as fundamental as Smith's. There had never been any question of a weakening of his faith: his position had been that of a child who asks a parent to be allowed to do something which he knows he should not do.

Doctor Bruin had said that the Commandant was not to receive the B1. God was apparently on Bruin's side. God and Doctor Bruin were the two persons—for Schiller entirely humanised his Deity—whom the young man *respected* most in the world. He had just come to realise that the Commandant was the one he *loved* the most.

He had decided in the circumstances that he must save him and risk, even invite, punishment if necessary. He had prayed and God had turned a deaf ear for reasons that only He knew.

Schiller now challenged Him. "I will give the Commandant the B1," he said, "and I will suffer any punishment that You think fit. Only Lord God," he added, "do not forget that I have been a good follower of Yours for a very long time— so be merciful in Your punishment. Do not make it too severe."

Schiller got out the little silver box that held the hypodermic apparatus and on his own skin he tested the needles to see which was the sharpest. Then he walked down towards the paling eastern sky, to the cookhouse, and got boiling water and sterilised the instrument. He felt happy and pleased with himself, strong and able to face squarely the wrath to come, both from Heaven and from Doctor Bruin.

The early morning air with the tang of wood smoke in it was fresh and even faintly cool. There was enough of the feeling of dawn in it to make Schiller remember the crisp, tart taste of the frosty wind at Ymuiden as it blew across the Zuider Zee.

Schiller was conscious that he had not slept all night. There was a tired, unbuttoned feeling in his limbs; but it was not unpleasant and he looked forward to getting a couple of hours sleep later, after the morning "pap" had been served. A friend of his in the cookhouse greeted him and gave him some hot sweet tea. He was grateful for it, though he realised the sugar in it must have been stolen out of the camp's daily ration.

Then he went back to the barrack. He picked up the vial of B1 from his bed-space, a little pot of alcohol and a wad of cotton-wool. Holding these in one hand and in the other the hypodermic syringe and needle, he moved down the barrack towards the Commandant's bed-space.

He carried the syringe needle forward and couched in his hand as the old steel-encased knights of the days of chivalry must have carried their lances when they went to do tourney on behalf of some woman they loved.

No one noticed him particularly as he passed, yet he felt that the whole barrack must be watching him.

He put the hypodermic down beside the old man's feet and went and fetched the hurricane lamp and set that there too.

He had realised that the Commandant would probably want to know why he, Schiller, was giving the injection rather than one of the doctors, and he was prepared to tell him that this kind of injection was better given in the very early morning.

As Schiller bent over the foot of the bed-space setting the things out, Wim passed behind him. The gangway was so narrow that he had to nudge his way past the orderly.

When he came back, after urinating again for perhaps the twentieth time, Schiller was still in the same position—only now he leaned forward over the bedding-boards with his hands widespread on them to support him. Wim playfully smacked the orderly's rump and moved on. He had not been able to see Schiller's face.

Had he been able to, he would have found it with a look of blank incredulity on it. Schiller had taken the Commandant's hand so as to waken the old man and help him move down the bed-space a little. It was quite inert and almost cold.

Schiller had not been able to believe his senses, but practice and routine had made his next action automatic. He had leaned over and turned the old man's head towards him. The eyes stared back at him unseeingly and the old man's mouth hung open.

It was that face that Schiller had been staring at when Wim had smacked him.

Schiller closed the dead man's eyes and pulled a cotton blanket over his head. Then, methodically, he took the syringe and the rest of the apparatus back to his bed-space. He went through all the motions of putting it away quite correctly.

Then he stood and shut his eyes. From deep inside himself he felt a great clenched fist rising.

He began softly, saying: "Thou hast cheated me. Thou hast killed him before I could reach him. Thou has taken him away. Deliberately. Perhaps. Thou thoughtst to teach me a lesson. And all that Thou has taught me is that Thou art capable of the same wretched meanness that Thou showest in Thy creature man." So it went on, and there seemed to be no end to it and no satisfaction in it.

Schiller did not know that as he cursed God, tears were running down his cheeks.

At last, the words that kept welling up within him froze. They were not done, they were like a shaft in his throat that grew solid and choked him.

With the B1 in his hands he went across to the Doctor's hut.

He saw Bruin sitting on the verandah outside, but though the Doctor sat almost next to him, he did not see Smith.

Schiller had not got his cap on; he was about to salute when he remembered this, so he came and stood to attention in front of Bruin and said through clenched teeth:

"The Commandant is dead." And handing over the vial,

"Here is the B1; I took it to give it to him; but I was cheated."

Then he turned on his heel and went away without another word and before Bruin could say anything in reply. The Doctor called after Schiller as he walked off, but the young man paid no heed.

Bruin shrugged and looked at the vial and sighed. "So he is dead. And Schiller has taken his death badly," he said, and as he heard himself say the words he felt an impulse, which he could barely restrain, to fling the vial on the ground and smash it to pieces. Instead he put it very gently on the seat beside him. Then he got up and turned and looked out across the strait to the next island. The sky was pale grey, beneath it the sea was an ochreous yellow. A faint flush of red touched the sky like the plumage at a pigeon's throat and already there was the heat of the sun in the air.

Smith said: "Schiller will get over it all right; he had God, but you, Bruin, who have nothing . . ."

Bruin did not bother to answer the implied question. He was thinking: this will pass over, this is not sorrow—there is no such thing as a sorrow, only a passing spasm that makes my nerves contract and makes me feel miserable. Unexpectedly he turned to the priest and said: "Pray for him, Padre." And then he felt shocked and dismayed with himself and turned and walked into the hut to get dressed so that he could go over and check Schiller's finding, though he had no doubt that it was correct.

While he dressed, he woke Van Reebek and told him of the Commandant's death. A little later both men left together to go over to the hospital barrack.

Smith went and bathed. When he came back, clean, and found that the room was empty, he did as Bruin had asked him to; he prayed for the Commandant. For the first time in his life he lost himself in his prayer. When at last he was finished he lay down and slept as one who has, just at the end of his strength, reached fulfilment.

CHAPTER II

DOCTOR BRUIN was walking back from the Commandant's burial. The cemetery was on a slight slope behind the camp cookhouse.

Earlier in the afternoon Jansen had also been buried there.

As he passed slowly through the camp, Bruin noticed that it was unusually quiet. It was normally the busiest time of the day, when the evening meal was being served and when the night shift was preparing to go out. Now, though there was the normal activity, it was all being carried out in a near silence.

As he walked, Bruin thought of Yoshimitsu's reaction to the deaths of the two men.

When he was told of Jansen's death, the Sergeant had sent at once for the Doctor and queried him about it. He was suspicious of the Doctor's diagnosis of heart failure. Yoshimitsu suggested that the chief cook might have been poisoned.

"But why should anyone want to poison the man?" Bruin had asked through the interpreter.

"He must have had many enemies in the camp," the Sergeant had replied. "He was too fat to have any friends among so many lean men."

"At a given moment," said Bruin, "the man's heart stopped beating. That surely is heart failure?"

Yoshimitsu stared at the Doctor for a long time with his narrow black eyes. Then he shrugged. "The man is dead," he said. "Who is taking his place?"

"The American, Burns."

"Why?" The question came sharply.

"Principally, because he is an honest man."

Yoshimitsu turned Bruin's reply over in his mind. "Tell him," he said at last, "to be careful. I do not like Americans."

The Sergeant had very little to say about the death of the Commandant. He had asked whether the B1 had been given to him. Bruin had told him that it had not.

"Who has it been given to?" Yoshimitsu had asked.

"To two younger men whose lives it will certainly save."

Yoshimitsu had frowned and turned and talked with Tadgibanu in Japanese. DeVissar had listened to the conversation and told Bruin, afterwards, that the Sergeant-Major had answered Yoshimitsu's complaint that the Doctor had deliberately disobeyed his order with the words, "He is a doctor and knows best what to do with medicines." He had also added, "It cannot always be easy to be a doctor."

The three Japanese, Nashimura, Tadgibanu and Yoshimitsu, had been at the graveside when the old man was buried. They had said nothing, but had saluted the coffin when everyone else did.

Bruin had thrown the first handful of earth and had felt a great melancholy as he did so, an unhappiness which had dragged at his throat and made him frown and look up at the tree-tops around the burial ground. It was a melancholy which he felt would stay with him for a long time.

Outside his billet, when he reached it, he found the man with the swollen mouth hovering, waiting for him.

"Well, what is it?" Bruin asked him without much interest. The man gave him another note. It read, "Mijnherr Doktor, I have been using warm salt-and-water on my mouth and it is a little better. Now, I beseech you, give me something that will make it quite better."

Bruin sighed, went into his billet and fetched some tablets. They were a preparation that was intended for chlorinating water and Bruin had been keeping them for himself in case he should ever have to drink anything foul or dangerous. They would, when dissolved, be but very little more effective than the salt water he had already prescribed, but they would give the man hope and the feeling of comfort that was to be had from the thought that he was being cared for.

"Take these, Jonge," he said, "they are the best I can do. Perhaps they will make it easier for you." And he explained how they should be used. The man had held the tablets cupped in his hands, high before his face, as if they had been diamonds. He was trembling in his excitement. He bowed his thanks several times and ran from the Doctor's hut back to his own, still carrying the tablets in his cupped hands.

Bruin watched him sadly until he was out of sight; then he turned and went into his own room. He lay down on his mat.

After a moment he picked up the black-covered exercise book again. He ran through the pages until he found, near the end, a part of it that he had read for the first time that morning.

". . . for another example," the old man had written, "at one of my hungriest periods, when my belly was nothing but an ache, I suddenly chanced on a couple of stems of climbing spinach. Someone had planted them and reared them in a little hidden corner behind a rubbish heap. Unfortunately for the owner, my hunger knew no conscience. There were perhaps thirty small leaves of spinach on the two plants. Before I picked them and stuffed them into my mouth, I paused, only momentarily, but I did pause to admire the beauty of the slender vein-coloured stems as they wound up the sticks, and the contrast that the heavily balanced, dark green leaves made against the stems and the light green background of the grass.

"So even amidst squalor and, at times, great need there have been glimpses of beauty. To have been no more than existing, even at such a low level, has not meant that life itself was entirely wasted.

"As prisoners of war, most of our civilised standards and principles have been uprooted, but though death has taken some fine men, and circumstances debased many others who might, under normal conditions, have been worthy enough, I have profited.

"If I wanted to strike an heroic attitude, I could say I have resolved the mystery of death. In actual fact, I have done nothing heroic. I have merely seen through it. Death as we know it is what we, mankind, have made it. We have made a garishly robed impostor of one of the greatest common-places in the universe. Death is only important because we give it importance. We die because we have invented death. It only has reality because we fear it and because we feel that we, as individuals, are too important to die. But, I repeat, there is no death. The seed never dies, but is immortal. For man's sake we must have faith in that seed, in its immortality and in its power, for the seed is indivisible from the Universe, though it is still no more than a seed, and the Universe is the greatest thing we know."

Bruin closed the book and held it in his hand.

The quick tropical twilight was dying. The features of the

room were fading; slowly darkness was filling it, expanding it, stretching out the space within it to meet the greater spaces of the night sky. 'Time and space are illimitable,' the Doctor thought, 'and I am but a man, a speck somewhere in the universe near the lower end of the scale between the sub-microscopic and the great charging masses of Neptune, Uranus and a million suns, some as big as the whole of our own solar system. To me, at this moment, my sadness is real, but only while I go on thinking of myself. When I let go and let myself think and fill with wonder, then I truly become part of this universal mystery, and in looking outwards at it I am happy because I have lost my identity, I am healed because I am no more. Once-a-man, now just a pair of eyes and an intelligence that makes me an interested spectator. I can still be happy and sad, still live in my skin, but I can escape it all too. I can be myself, and the next minute I can be all-men, and beyond-men. I have added a new depth to myself, a depth that is not out of place alongside the greatest profundity of all, infinity.'

2

The Korean in the lighter had been suffering for some days with a sickness brought on by drinking too much raw alcohol. He had a dull headache and an evil humour.

The Dutchman nearest him in the crowded pack of humanity that was going over to relieve the night shift had contrived to give the scowling guard elbow-room. But the lighter jolted as it struck the quayside and threw him against the man, who promptly rounded on him and slapped his face.

The Dutchman tried to explain in Malay that the push had been accidental. The Korean, who did not speak Malay, assumed that the man was trying to make excuses and saw that he was afraid and cringing. Like a dog that obeys one of nature's laws in killing off a weaker creature, the Korean became excited by the Dutchman's fear and attacked him savagely.

The Dutch officer in charge of the group was not a regular soldier but a prosperous businessman who, on being called up, had used his contacts in high places to get himself a commission.

He volunteered to go out with the working-parties fairly

regularly, which showed an enterprise that was lacking in many of the other officers, but it was prompted by the same instinct that would in civil life have inclined him to take a chance in a highly competitive market. In both cases the risks were greater but the dividends compensatingly higher. In this case the dividends were food. Beside the higher working-party ration, the officer, who by camp standards was a rich man, could buy things for himself from the coolies.

In addition to being a rich man, the officer had two obvious traits of character: he was humane and a physical coward. They were traits which warred within him whenever one of his men was being beaten. His cowardice always won.

So while his compatriot was being savaged at the other end of the lighter he made no move to interfere.

The men in the lighter muttered against him, comparing him unfavourably with Van Reebek. Even though the men knew that an officer's intervention would often be unavailing, his interference would show courage, which heartened them and gave them confidence in him.

Several of the men in the boat nearest the officer made as if to open a gangway through their ranks, inviting him to pass forward to the site of the trouble. With a blandness he was far from feeling, the officer shook his head and announced that there was nothing he could do.

Other Koreans on the quay soon began to shout at the man in the landing barge, telling him that he had beaten the man enough and that he was holding up disembarkation. The Dutchman who was being beaten was cowering against the boat's side, doubling himself up and thereby increasing the Korean's scorn for him and inviting more punishment.

Contemptuously the Korean kicked the man viciously with the toe of his boot, connecting painfully with his victim's os coccyx. The Dutchman fell grovelling at the Korean's feet. The guard shrugged, spat and, feeling better than he had done for several days, climbed out of the barge on to the quay and walked off towards the village at the head of it.

The men in the barge followed him out and waited in an untidy group to be fallen in and marched to work as Van Reebek and other officers did whenever they took them over. Marching gave them a sense of solidarity and purpose; but as the guards did not insist upon it, the officer who was with them today did not either. He knew he had not a military manner with his words of command and therefore shirked the issue, explaining it away by saying that there was no sense, under the circumstances of military defeat, to go on playing at soldiers.

He waved to the men to carry on and they straggled away up the quay towards the airfield.

The officer went to the man who had been beaten and apologised for not having come to his assistance.

"I am not a very brave man," he said, "but I have got a little money. Perhaps five dollars will help you to forget your pains."

The man had not been badly hurt except by the Korean's last contemptuous kick. He took the money insolently and turned his back on the officer, who shrugged at the man's lack of gratitude and then followed at the rear of the column as it moved forward, his conscience freed of any sense of debt.

Van Reebek, who had seen the party off at the guard-house as the old Commandant had always done when he was fit enough, watched the men straggling away off the quay on the other side of the water. He wondered how he was going to be able to check the officer in charge of the party and make him march his men to their work properly. The ex-business-man was almost twice Van Reebek's age and a city alderman in the big town in which he had lived before the war.

Then Van Reebek reflected that he now had the power to stop the man going out with the working-parties altogether unless he looked after his troops properly. That would probably be sufficient to make him behave correctly.

The Lieutenant turned and walked up to the cookhouse for a word with Burns about the day's rations.

He found the American stoking the cookhouse fires himself, and asked what had happened to the two men whose job it should have been.

"The bastards won't work for me, Lootenant," was the reply.

Van Reebek went and fetched the two men of out the billet. In front of Burns he dismissed them from the cook-house staff and told them to report for duty with that evening's shift to go to the airfield. He then called the rest of the cook-house staff together and warned them that they would be as summarily dealt with if they did not carry out Burns' orders.

The men listened sullenly and one of their number started to argue. Van Reebek walked over and stood immediately in front of the man. The Lieutenant's height and his conviction that he was right lent him authority.

Quietly he told the man he was prepared to remove every man then working in the cookhouse and to replace them all if they felt they could not work for Burns. Every man there was replaceable, he reminded them; there was not a fit man in the camp who would not be eager to come in and take over the work.

The man he was talking to continued to argue, saying that most of the men in the camp were Dutch and that it was only right that the man in charge of the kitchens should be Dutch too.

"So you will not work for Mijnheer Burns?"

The man looked at the ground. There was a long silence. Van Reebek broke it, saying:

"Not only will you work for him, but if I hear the least complaint about you from him, you will go out—do you understand? And that applies to you all." He looked angrily along the line. "Now get back to your work."

After Van Reebek had left the cookhouse, Martin, the Englishman, went to Burns and said: "Blimey, mate, we've got a real officer type in charge, eh? Scotched that bugger proper, 'ee did. What jer fink of 'im, eh?"

Burns was guarded. "I guess it's something to do with being a new broom," he said, "though, by Jesus, it's going to make my work a lot easier if he can make them step in line when they are told."

In the Doctor's billet Van Reebek was lying on his bed. His bruised face throbbed from his previous day's beating and he was feeling the weight of his responsibilities very heavily upon him. He had been lying there for about half an hour, when Doctor Bruin came in.

He looked at the young officer with an amused expression.

"So you have turned the cookhouse upside down already?" he asked.

"Oh, damn," said Van Reebek, "but I couldn't help it. If we are going to have Burns in there, they must obey him."

Bruin continued to smile. "True," he said, "and you as well have got to make your authority felt."

He paused. Then he added, "But you are doing all right. Some of them are calling you the Commandant already. There is plenty of time to convert others to the same opinion. All the time in the world, in fact, for I see in the paper you brought that Von Runstedt has made a successful breakthrough. The war may go on for years."